Sabotage in the Sky

SELECTED FICTION WORKS BY L. RON HUBBARD

FANTASY
The Case of the Friendly Corpse
Death's Deputy
Fear
The Ghoul
The Indigestible Triton
Slaves of Sleep & The Masters of Sleep
Typewriter in the Sky
The Ultimate Adventure

SCIENCE FICTION
Battlefield Earth
The Conquest of Space
The End Is Not Yet
Final Blackout
The Kilkenny Cats
The Kingslayer
The Mission Earth Dekalogy*
Ole Doc Methuselah
To the Stars

ADVENTURE
The Hell Job series

WESTERN
Buckskin Brigades
Empty Saddles
Guns of Mark Jardine
Hot Lead Payoff

A full list of L. Ron Hubbard's
novellas and short stories is provided at the back.

*Dekalogy—a group of ten volumes

L. RON HUBBARD

Sabotage
in the Sky

GALAXY
PRESS

Published by
Galaxy Press, LLC
7051 Hollywood Boulevard, Suite 200
Hollywood, CA 90028

Printed in the United States of America.

ISBN-10 1-59212-297-3
ISBN-13 978-1-59212-297-4

Library of Congress Control Number: 2007927532

Contents

Stories from Pulp Fiction's Golden Age

A ND it *was* a golden age.
The 1930s and 1940s were a vibrant, seminal time for a gigantic audience of eager readers, probably the largest per capita audience of readers in American history. The magazine racks were chock-full of publications with ragged trims, garish cover art, cheap brown pulp paper, low cover prices—and the most excitement you could hold in your hands.

"Pulp" magazines, named for their rough-cut, pulpwood paper, were a vehicle for more amazing tales than Scheherazade could have told in a million and one nights. Set apart from higher-class "slick" magazines, printed on fancy glossy paper with quality artwork and superior production values, the pulps were for the "rest of us," adventure story after adventure story for people who liked to *read*. Pulp fiction authors were no-holds-barred entertainers—real storytellers. They were more interested in a thrilling plot twist, a horrific villain or a white-knuckle adventure than they were in lavish prose or convoluted metaphors.

The sheer volume of tales released during this wondrous golden age remains unmatched in any other period of literary history—hundreds of thousands of published stories in over nine hundred different magazines. Some titles lasted only an issue or two; many magazines succumbed to paper shortages during World War II, while others endured for decades yet. Pulp fiction remains as a treasure trove of stories you can read, stories you can love, stories you can remember. The stories were driven by plot and character, with grand heroes, terrible villains, beautiful damsels (often in distress), diabolical plots, amazing places, breathless romances. The readers wanted to be taken beyond the mundane, to live adventures far removed from their ordinary lives—and the pulps rarely failed to deliver.

In that regard, pulp fiction stands in the tradition of all memorable literature. For as history has shown, good stories are much more than fancy prose. William Shakespeare, Charles Dickens, Jules Verne, Alexandre Dumas—many of the greatest literary figures wrote their fiction for the readers, not simply literary colleagues and academic admirers. And writers for pulp magazines were no exception. These publications reached an audience that dwarfed the circulations of today's short story magazines. Issues of the pulps were scooped up and read by over thirty million avid readers each month.

Because pulp fiction writers were often paid no more than a cent a word, they had to become prolific or starve. They also had to write aggressively. As Richard Kyle, publisher and editor of *Argosy,* the first and most long-lived of the pulps, so pointedly explained: "The pulp magazine writers, the best of them, worked for markets that did not write for critics or attempt to satisfy timid advertisers. Not having to answer to anyone other than their readers, they wrote about human beings on the edges of the unknown, in those new lands the future would explore. They wrote for what we would become, not for what we had already been."

Some of the more lasting names that graced the pulps include H. P. Lovecraft, Edgar Rice Burroughs, Robert E. Howard, Max Brand, Louis L'Amour, Elmore Leonard, Dashiell Hammett, Raymond Chandler, Erle Stanley Gardner, John D. MacDonald, Ray Bradbury, Isaac Asimov, Robert Heinlein—and, of course, L. Ron Hubbard.

In a word, he was among the most prolific and popular writers of the era. He was also the most enduring—hence this series—and certainly among the most legendary. It all began only months after he first tried his hand at fiction, with L. Ron Hubbard tales appearing in *Thrilling Adventures*, *Argosy*, *Five-Novels Monthly*, *Detective Fiction Weekly*, *Top-Notch*, *Texas Ranger*, *War Birds*, *Western Stories*, even *Romantic Range*. He could write on any subject, in any genre, from jungle explorers to deep-sea divers, from G-men and gangsters, cowboys and flying aces to mountain climbers, hard-boiled detectives and spies. But he really began to shine when he turned his talent to science fiction and fantasy of which he authored nearly fifty novels or novelettes to forever change the shape of those genres.

Following in the tradition of such famed authors as Herman Melville, Mark Twain, Jack London and Ernest Hemingway, Ron Hubbard actually lived adventures that his own characters would have admired—as an ethnologist among primitive tribes, as prospector and engineer in hostile climes, as a captain of vessels on four oceans. He even wrote a series of articles for *Argosy*, called "Hell Job," in which he lived and told of the most dangerous professions a man could put his hand to.

Finally, and just for good measure, he was also an accomplished photographer, artist, filmmaker, musician and educator. But he was first and foremost a *writer*, and that's the L. Ron Hubbard we come to know through the pages of this volume.

This library of Stories from the Golden Age presents the best of L. Ron Hubbard's fiction from the heyday of storytelling, the Golden Age of the pulp magazines. In these eighty volumes, readers are treated to a full banquet of 153 stories, a kaleidoscope of tales representing every imaginable genre: science fiction, fantasy, western, mystery, thriller, horror, even romance—action of all kinds and in all places.

Because the pulps themselves were printed on such inexpensive paper with high acid content, issues were not meant to endure. As the years go by, the original issues of every pulp from *Argosy* through *Zeppelin Stories* continue crumbling into brittle, brown dust. This library preserves the L. Ron Hubbard tales from that era, presented with a distinctive look that brings back the nostalgic flavor of those times.

L. Ron Hubbard's Stories from the Golden Age has something for every taste, every reader. These tales will return you to a time when fiction was good clean entertainment and the most fun a kid could have on a rainy afternoon or the best thing an adult could enjoy after a long day at work.

Pick up a volume, and remember what reading is supposed to be all about. Remember curling up with a *great story.*

—Kevin J. Anderson

KEVIN J. ANDERSON *is the author of more than ninety critically acclaimed works of speculative fiction, including The Saga of Seven Suns, the continuation of the Dune Chronicles with Brian Herbert, and his* New York Times *bestselling novelization of L. Ron Hubbard's* Ai! Pedrito!

Sabotage in the Sky

Sabotage in the Sky

E RICH VON STRAUB resembled very little the stiff Nazi officer who had, so recently, clicked his heels and bowed shortly to the Minister of the Air in Berlin. Then his manner had been perfectly Prussian.

The Minister of the Air in Berlin had said, "Colonel, according to your record, you studied aeronautical engineering in the United States and you speak the language and know the country. We have a great deal of faith in you. I have had you report here to inform you that you are leaving, via Italy, with properly forged passports and birth certificates, for the United States."

"Yes, sir," said von Straub.

"The English and the French are depending on the planes of the United States to achieve their air supremacy. Already we have a sufficient number of agents at work in United States aircraft plants, but they are watched so closely that they can do very little. You, Colonel, have always been a man of resource and intelligence."

"Thank you, sir."

"You understand that unless this flow of superior planes is at least hampered, we cannot long hope to continue victorious in the sky. We believe that the best method of hampering this flow of planes is to influence English and French opinion

3

of them. Soon we will have the Messerschmitt 118D for pursuit. It has been brought to us that the United States has, in experimental condition, the one plane which will defeat the Messerschmitt 118D. One other plane is nearly equal to it. The British and French are trying to buy these two types of ship. If those planes convince the British and French that they are superior, the manufacture of the Messerschmitt 118D will be reduced in importance. But, Colonel, you are a resourceful man.

"We are not tampering with our production of the Messerschmitt 118D. We will depend upon you to keep the British and French from buying either of these two American planes and then, because 118D is a secret we will maintain with our lives, we will suddenly be able to take over the sky from the English, sweep their isles, down their retaliating bombers, and so bring victory to our glorious cause.

"If you can arrange to convince the English and French that these two American planes are neither safe nor fast, you will find yourself a hero in your own land. Failing that, you will deliver to us a complete plane of each type. Ample funds are at your disposal. The lives of your brother officers depend upon you, so work well!"

"Heil Hitler!" von Straub piously said, turning sharply and marching away.

But Erich von Straub, a man of resource and intelligence, did not at all resemble Albert Straud who had, very recently, been hired as an aviation mechanic by Beryl-Cannard Airlines. Albert Straud was obviously a Teuton, but then so are a large percent of the employees of all aircraft companies in the United States. His blond hair was curly and his eyes were mild and of an innocent blue; he was of medium stature and only passingly handsome; his bearing had no suggestion of the military, but leaned rather into careless ease. He was cheerful and conversational and helpful and, in fact, lived up completely to the fine letters of recommendation he had brought—letters which had been taken from a Boeing man who had somehow managed to get himself killed in an automobile crash.

He stood just now, this Albert Straud, on the apron of the BCA plant's second hangar and scanned, with a fellow employee, the murky heights of the southern sky—for BCA is only thirty miles from Washington, DC, and shares Washington, DC's climate.

There was a flash of silver up there and a powerful engine became loud so suddenly that it sounded more like an explosion than an approaching plane. Abruptly the roar stopped. The silver became a low-wing monoplane, stabbing down at the field. And nearly every man on the BCA property froze, drop-jawed and unbreathing.

Planes landing there were too common to be remarked. But two things were different about this ship. One was that it was coming in upside down, and the other, that it probably contained one Bill Trevillian, absent from these parts for nearly four years.

Straight down the runway streaked the ship, the pilot seemingly wholly undisturbed by this reversal of the average state of scenery. And then, almost at the stalling point, when it seemed that he must inevitably crash, he snap rolled! And when the plane's landing gear was under it where it should have been all the time, the wheels were also being rotated by an instantaneous contact with earth.

There was a furious geyser of dust at the runway's end and the field was full of a joyous bellow of power—and the silver ship nearly took off again, headed toward the hangars. Another cloud, then the sputter of a cut motor, and there sat the plane, parked neatly on the line, in between two fighting planes, almost touching wings on either side.

"Well, well, well!" said Albert Straud. "I have not seen that since the great Udet. Any idea who the pilot might be?"

His companion, a stocky fellow with a wise eye and a mouth full of tobacco, namely Greasy Hannagan, spat and drawled, "You evidently ain't never seen Bill Trevillian before, buddy. Him and Udet used to pick handkerchiefs out of the breast pockets of each other's Sunday suits with their wing tips."

"Bill Trevillian? Oh, yes. The racing pilot. I should like to know him."

"You'll know him all right, buddy. You and me is goin' to be his repair crew. He's up here from Mexico to take charge of the BCA 41 Pursuit."

"Ah. So they've been waiting for him before they tried it again."

"Yeah. They been waiting for him. Hello, Bill, you old scatter-wit!"

"'Lo, Greasy. You wouldn't be putting on weight, would you?"

"Hell," said Greasy, "what's the difference? Ain't like it used to be, conserving the payload. How you been?"

Bill Trevillian had eased half out of the pit and sat now on the turtleback, his long, booted legs dangling, while he untangled himself from his radio helmet and oxygen mask. He was good-looking in a sleepy sort of way, very tall, very languid, always looking for something upon which to lean his obviously weary soul. Down in his eyes there lay a watchful spark of humor, and upon his lips there always lingered the ghost of his last smile and the beginning of the next.

Bill slid down and looked at Greasy. "Been a long time, huh?" he drawled.

"Four years," said Greasy. "Where you been?"

"Oh," said Bill vaguely, "France, Africa, Mexico. Lots of the best bars, Greasy."

"I hear you were practically rebuilding the Mexican air force," said Greasy.

"The report," yawned Bill, "has been grossly exaggerated. Where's the boss?"

"Cannard is over at Operations," said Greasy.

"You my crew?" said Bill.

"Sure. I hadda lick six guys when we heard you was goin' to work for us again, but I got it, no matter how hard I tried to get out of it. This here is the guy that's been workin' with me. He's a whiz on engines. He quotes poetry to 'em or something. Name of Albert Straud."

Bill looked at Straud and nodded, instantly reserved, not because he saw anything to distrust about Straud, but because Bill was very shy.

"Very pleased," said Albert Straud with a short handshake. "I hope I can please you."

7

"Please the plane and you'll please me," said Bill. "Now listen, Greasy, this is *Irma*. She was built out of four planes and a truck, and she runs exclusively on tequila. Cold cream her, and take the wave out of her tach, and tighten up her left aileron control. She's fast, but she's temperamental, and she's so jealous of me that she tried to kill the last guy that flew her."

"Okay," said Greasy, spitting hugely on the tarmac. He then put his hand on *Irma*'s turtleback and probably would have said something bawdy to her, but a roaring engine suddenly made all speech impossible.

Heads went up and the plane came down. It had cut in to the field past the usual high-tension wires. Evidently it had been flying ten feet above the housetops, for no one had seen it or heard it until it verticaled into the field. Now it shot outward, snapped into a bank which brought its nose to the wind, and slashed with cut gun down the long stretch of concrete.

Suddenly the ship skidded to get away from the runway and, leveling out, began to float for a landing. And with one voice, spectators gasped, "The wheels are up!"

Like a bird with its feet tucked up against its body, and seemingly with no effort to put them down, the plane closed the few gapping inches between itself and earth. The engine stopped completely. There came a rending scream of lacerated metal, and dust ballooned skyward, completely hiding the plane.

A crash siren wailed. People began yelling and sprinting. Cars with men on their running boards curved out toward the dust. A fire engine, with asbestos-clad "hot papas" gleamingly apparent upon it, jangled and clanged toward the crash.

But few knew exactly where, in all that dust, the plane had stopped or just how badly it had wrecked itself. It had come to rest about a hundred yards from Bill, and as he was to windward of it, all was plain.

Fearing that the small white tongues of fire might come dancing out from under the cowl at any instant, Bill loped to the side of the ship and wrestled with the hood until he got it open. And by that time it was certain that the plane would not burn.

Two black hands were lifted to black and opaque goggles. The dripping black face became startling as soon as the goggles were raised, for there were white areas, then, about the eyes. A fine spray of oil from a broken line was still bathing the pilot, but the slippery hands could not seem to get any grasp on the belt. Bill unhooked the belt and helped the pilot out.

The danger was over. The ship was only slightly hurt. And the sight of those two white-rimmed eyes in that jet face made Bill—unfortunate Bill—grin.

"Go ahead and grin, you big ape!" snapped the pilot.

And then Bill—poor, unfortunate Bill—*did* grin. The pilot was a girl. And her voice had so much challenging ferocity and she looked so funny, standing there about five feet two and threatening him, that Bill guffawed. And after all the nervous tension of expecting to see somebody fried alive, he couldn't stop guffawing. He sank down on the wing, while fire engines and ambulances—all disappointment now—yowled to a halt and raised more dust.

Bill kept on laughing, for the more he laughed the madder she got, and the madder she got the funnier she looked. No one can glare properly when completely inked with oil.

She stomped away to the ambulance, and when the intern tried to help her in she angrily thrust him aside and, taking the sheet off the stretcher, began to wipe her face. She was getting primed for battle and her big sky-blue eyes were full of the lust to kill. But some helping hand had already thrust Bill away from the plane, and so her quarry was lost. Grimly vowing nothing short of the Chinese rat torture, she hung on to a car and so was taken to Operations.

Bill was still chuckling as he finished his instructions to Greasy. And then, "Leave it to a woman, Greasy. No wheels." And again Bill was laughing.

"Maybe something happened to her wheels," said Greasy.

"Oh, that's not possible," said Albert Straud quickly—a shade too quickly. But he rapidly amended that error. "I have been hearing that those L97s were very good pursuits."

"L97?" said Bill. "What a flock of new ships there are that I don't know anything about at all!"

"It's an X job," said Greasy. "Newest thing in pursuits."

Straud was already too interested in *Irma* to hear.

"The only thing," added Greasy, "which'll come close to it is this here BCA 41 Pursuit."

"What's a dame doing with a hot crate like that? And an X job, too?" demanded Bill.

Greasy would have answered, but a messenger came from

Cannard asking Bill to come over to the office, and so Bill, forgetting about it, slouched along after the boy.

Cannard was surrounded by silver airplane cigarette lighters and a photo-mosaic of the plant and mahogany furniture and Persian rugs and expensive cigars. It was super-modernistic and indicated the affluence which had descended upon BCA with the breakdown of international diplomacy.

Cannard was a lean, nervous fellow with a trick of stabbing people with voice and eyes, of answering questions before they were asked, and getting angry at things which didn't exist, and pointing with pride and flaming with indignation only split seconds apart. He was the soul and nerves of BCA, and he seemed to think that BCA planes flew only because his own willpower held them up, despite anything his engineers might say or plan.

"Hello, Trevillian. Have a seat, Bill. Glad to see you back. Sit down and have a cigarette. Well, how was Mexico?"

But before Bill could answer that, Cannard was making a wide circuit of the room, pointing to production and profit charts and laying out BCA business the way a machine gunner lays out an enemy charge.

Bill knew all about this. He sat down on the arm of a chair and slumped into it (he never was known to sit straight in a chair, but always across it) and swung his battered boots indolently, looking interested through force of habit, but really wondering if Mamie's up the road still put out a good hamburger.

"So there you have it," said Cannard. "Hundreds of planes ordered. Six new ships experimental. Millions rolling in. And the tooling of the plant may bankrupt us. And the British and French are aching to see our 41 tested, and you are the man who is going to do it."

"What I can't savvy," said Bill, swinging his battered boots and gazing sleepily at his cigarette, "is why you sent all the way to Mexico for me. Aren't there any test pilots left or did they all drink themselves to death?"

"Bill, you know pursuits. For years and years you've known hot ships. You're aces. You've got a name. It's an asset."

"And the real reason?" said Bill.

"You've trained the pursuit pilots into the last wrinkles in three armies. You've slammed the hottest planes ever built to first in the hottest races ever flown. You know all there is to know about pursuit, stunts, fast ships—"

"And now the point," smiled Bill.

"Well"—Cannard nervously leaped into his chair and shook a finger at Bill—"the point is, we've lost two test pilots in a month. You'll find it out quick enough, so I'll tell you."

"Thought a salary like three thousand a month looked grossly exaggerated!" said Bill.

"But they weren't as good as you are—"

"Both killed on the BCA 41," said Bill.

"Yes. How did you know?"

"Why, you are offering me three thousand a month to test it, aren't you? And a bonus of ten thousand for successful demonstration to foreign buyers!"

"Trevillian, we've always been friends. Bill, you were brought up with BCA. We know that you—"

"Aw," said Bill, "I know already that I'm the best flyer that ever flew. I'm half-eagle and half-balloon. I've got ailerons for thumbs and flippers instead of toes. But listen, Cannard, if I test BCA 41 I'm just an ordinary son of a gun that sometimes can tell the difference between a prop and a hangar—and if you expect miracles—"

"No, no, Bill! It's a swell ship. It's okay."

"Then," said Bill, swinging his battered boots, "why did it kill two men?"

"Well—hell's skyways, Bill, you always were the orneriest drink of water to talk to in the whole game! Be human! I'm on a spot. We've got to test BCA 41. Okay. We've got to sell her because our BCA 35 is already obsolete. The Messerschmitt 109F can fly rings around it. But we were tooled for thousands of them, and we've got to have a ship to replace it. Unless we're in production on BCA 41 in one month, we're broke. There's the honest story. Our bombers have had three cancellations because Lockheed suddenly trebled production and sucked in the orders that should have been ours. We're in debt to here, understand? And if you won't test BCA 41 we're sunk!"

"That's it, appeal to my old loyalty to BCA, Cannard. Answer me one question straight."

"Sure. Sure, Bill."

"Cannard, do you ever recall—now answer this honestly—do you ever recall telling the truth once in your whole life?"

"Aw, now, Bill!" For Cannard was alarmed at the way Bill was moving toward the door.

"I haven't refused, have I?" said Bill.

"You'll take it?" Cannard cried.

"I'll take it," drawled Bill.

13

He had opened the door a little and it was left open while he swiftly changed the subject to avoid further praise.

"Say, Cannard, a pursuit job just came in out there. A girl flying it. I believe it's an L97—whatever *that* is. How come?"

"Well, I can't refuse the field," said Cannard. "It's a public field. And besides, she's a good kid, even if she did get engine trouble and have to land here."

"Engine trouble?" said Bill.

"Sure. She's a good pilot. She's—"

"Yeah," said Bill. "Yeah, she's a swell pilot. Doesn't know enough to put down her wheels! All dames are alike, Cannard. They're daffy in the switchbox!"

"But her reputation—" began Cannard.

"Has probably been grossly exaggerated," said Bill. And he started out.

The pilot of the L97 was standing at the weather desk in the outer office, viciously busy with a map which she held upside down. She was still smeared with oil from helmet crown to battered boots.

Bill paused long enough to turn the map around for her, and then wandered out to the field. . . .

At five o'clock that evening, as usual, workmen streamed through the gates in a weary river, having been duly showered and inspected. As the flow dispersed to the parking lot and the street and the buses, one man, Albert Straud, detached himself from his companions and unobtrusively eased into a cigar store.

"Hello," he said cheerfully to the clerk. "A pack of humps and some change for the phone."

14

The clerk, quickly producing the cigarettes and the change, could not resist smiling back. "Looks like it's going to get hotter, don't it?"

"Hotter before it gets colder," grinned Albert Straud. "Thanks."

He went into a phone booth and dialed long distance, asking for Calver, Maryland, and the number of a pay phone there. He glanced at his wristwatch to make certain he had timed his contact properly. He had. He deposited the quarters required.

"Hello, John?" said Albert. "This is George."

"How are you, George?"

"Not feeling so well. Saw a crash today and for a moment I thought it was going to be serious."

"That's too bad. How serious was it?"

And suddenly Albert, seeing he was alone in this string of booths, let his rage go. "Scratched some paint. Broke an oil line. You bungling *fool*!"

"I . . . I did all—"

"And L97 is still in flying condition! If I hadn't been on the field Kip Lee chose to land upon, I suppose you wouldn't have reported your failure at all! You stupid clod! Do orders mean nothing to you?"

"I jammed the landing gear all right, sir. It couldn't have worked—"

"It didn't work . . . but that wasn't enough! When you get your hands on that ship again . . . Somebody is coming. Well, John, I'm certainly glad to hear you're feeling better. Be careful not to get sick again. You know what the doctor said . . . the

15

next time it may be fatal. . . . Yes, I'm taking care of him. Yes. Well . . . be seeing you, John."

"Honest-to-God, sir, I didn't mean to slip up—"

"And give my best to your wife," said Albert. He hung up.

When he stepped from the booth, the clerk smiled at him again. "Yessir, it sure looks like it's getting hotter."

"Yes, it sure does," said Albert. "Well, don't take any wooden nickels." And humming a little song, he sauntered out.

That night, Bill, in Greasy's roadster, went to Washington. It was a very natural thing for Bill to do, for he was welcome in any embassy and he had only to pick out the one which was throwing a ball that night and then pick out his dress suit from his baggage and roll.

He was in a very happy frame of mind, despite his present job—for Bill was the sort who lasted a long time, and only pilots who never worry last. He rode along whistling badly off key and driving very, very cautiously—which is also a pilot trait—and only occasionally cursing the motorists who suicidally flipped by. He had flown only two thousand miles the day before and three thousand on this day, and he had had a full hour's rest at the bungalow of Happy Daye, where he had been invited to park that afternoon.

When he got to the embassy, having navigated innumerable circles and "no left turns," he had a sudden feeling, a premonition, that he was about to enter upon an adventure of some sort. He was not sure what, but only that it would be something nice—not anything humdrum, like breaking his neck.

He was ushered through the glittering rooms and halls, hailed here and there, past groups of bemedaled diplomats, sparkling officers and predatory women, to the bar, where he fortified himself with two drinks of his own concoction which he called a "Flaming Coffin" and which always set bartenders on edge, the suspense of watching for him to explode was so terrible.

Half a dozen air officers of various ranks and nations collected about him and began congratulating him upon the job he had finished in Mexico—which Bill assured them was grossly exaggerated. He had them served several of his "Flaming Coffins" and was forced, shortly after, to go prowling in search of people who could still talk and walk.

And then his adventure happened. A man in the uniform of the United States Air Service, wearing the stars of a general, eased toward him to cut him off. And on the general's arm was a young lady who— Well, Bill just stopped.

"Trevillian, old boy," said the general, "my young friend has been in a flat spin ever since you walked in the door and I've been recruited to do the introductions. Miss Lee, may I introduce Bill Trevillian. And don't say I didn't warn you."

Bill bowed, staring. For Miss Lee was something upon which a man could stare for hours on end and still be stunned. Her hair, sweeping down in a cascade of yellow to her creamy bare shoulders, made one's hands twitch. Her fragile little face—too small, it seemed, to hold her gigantic sky-blue eyes—was something to drive a poet into paralysis from sheer wordlessness. She was about five feet two and slender as a boy, and so light that one became afraid to touch her for fear

17

she would break. Her evening gown, what there was of it, was white satin, and it was apparently supported by miracles.

"Oh, Mr. Trevillian," said Miss Lee, and her voice was such a soothing caress it would have turned snarling wolves into fawning lapdogs.

Somehow the general managed to vanish.

"Dance?" said Bill, swallowing hard and still staring.

"Please," said Miss Lee.

They danced. They didn't say a word. They just danced and the music was only for them and the ballroom was an endless vista of altocirrus. For Bill could dance—and Miss Lee could dance!

Someone tittered and they found they had been dancing for seconds after the music had stopped. But even then they were not confused or even brought to earth.

"Balcony?" said Bill, still staring.

"Balcony," said Miss Lee.

And they went out and stood upon the balcony, with the spring zephyr in her hair and pressing her gown against her, and Bill put his arm about her so she would not be cold.

They looked at the lighted Capitol dome, which was a mound of white ice cream under the stars. They looked at the Washington Monument, an upright icicle topped with tiny spots of red, and decided that Washington was beautiful.

And then Bill began to tell her about himself: what a lonely life he had led, and how cold and alone it was up there in the sky, and how swift, clean wings soared against the flame of far dawns.

"I . . . I've never flown," said Miss Lee.

"Huh? You've never . . . Gosh! Look . . . I've got a car. I'll take you out to BCA. And . . . look . . . there's the moon. We'll fly straight up into it, just you and me, and leave all this behind us."

"Oh, Mr. Trevillian!"

Bill, for all his sleepy languor, was a man of action on occasion. In less than an hour they were having a grumbling night crew roll *Irma* out on the apron and Bill was putting a flying jacket (it had the double eagles of Mexico embroidered in gold upon it and was much stained with use) about her slim shoulders and felt that if he didn't own the world, he at least held a mortgage on most of it.

He put her into the front cockpit as one might set an invaluable carving into its carefully padded box.

"Now look," said Bill. "I haven't disconnected the controls and I shouldn't be flying with the duals still in, but you just keep your feet away from those rudder bars and your hands away from the stick and all will be well."

She appeared slightly frightened, but he soothed her and said there was nothing about which to be afraid, that *Irma* was the best ship ever, even if her ancestry had been grossly exaggerated.

And then they took off.

Irma sent the field, rows of trees, car-lit roads and a sparkling stream fleeing behind them, and with the bright disc of her prop bellowing into the night, stabbed upward at the moon.

Up, up, up, until cities were patches of blurred yellow and the stars were so bright, despite the moon, that they looked like the ornaments on a dowager's neck. Up, up, up, until the moon was an enormous coin just within reach, and it seemed that they would leave the world entirely and just soar forever in outer space.

Miss Lee seemed to be taking it well, thought Bill. She was a swell kid. She was the best ever. And he felt so masterful and protective that he almost burst.

But at last he had to stop climbing and start down.

He cut the gun, only blipping the engine occasionally to keep it warm, and the whistle of wind in the wings made the night seem mysterious and lonely.

But Bill, for all his protective urge, would not have been Bill Trevillian if he hadn't decided he really ought to snap roll a time or two. He did. And then he thought it might be a good idea to fly for a little way upon their back, just to show the girl how things looked in reverse, for it isn't everyone who can stand the Washington Monument and the Capitol dome—both visible, but far away—on their tops.

Upside down. And now Bill pointed *Irma*'s nose at the field where they had now put on the floods. The girl seemed to be taking it well, up there in the front cockpit. No hands in sight gripping the coaming.

Well, he'd fly straight and not try a stunt landing. And with a touch of stick and a little rudder to steady—Ye Gods!

Bill felt himself go white. There was something wrong! The controls were like permanent fixtures! Neither rudder would give. Neither to the left nor the right could he move that stick! Frozen controls! Neither forward nor backward—!

And there was that brilliant field, its runways glaringly

white in the pattern of wheel spokes. There was the lighted T—there were the hangars! Closer and closer!

He strove to cut the engine, but that, too, was beyond touch. The throttle would not move!

Closer and closer—that white pattern larger and larger and *Irma* making full speed—three hundred and ten miles an hour—

Bill prayed with sudden, unaccustomed fervor and fury. He tried to break the controls loose. He cursed every nut and bolt in the ship.

And up came the field—three hundred and ten miles an hour!

He could feel the sweat starting out all over him. What a flaming crash this would be! And that poor kid up front—! Her first ride—

It was a matter of only seconds. The field was about to be splattered with flaming chips of a onetime ship!

Abruptly, things happened. Seemingly of her own accord, *Irma* flipped over and upright and the gun was cut. *Irma*'s wheels reached for earth. *Irma* fishtailed and lost her speed. There was a welcome rumble of wheels on concrete—

They were down—safely!

Weakly, Bill ground looped and taxied toward the hangar as the field floods went off. Good old *Irma*! But how the devil—?

He braked her on the apron and pushed back the hood. Very gently he reached into Miss Lee's cockpit, expecting to find her in a state of collapse.

"Oh, Mr. Trevillian! That was marvelous!"

"Yeah," said Bill. "Yeah. I guess . . . I guess I better take you home!"

It was warm on the dirt testing field of Lee Aircraft, Calver, Maryland. A few mechanics were crawling over the L97, which lay, much bruised, on the floor of the shop, having been hauled there in the small hours by a truck. She was now minus her complete landing assembly, which was being carefully checked, while other men replaced the dented and ripped plates under the fuselage and fitted a new prop to the engine. Over at one side, the other L97 was on the verge of completion, but the crew at Lee Aircraft was so small that both activities could not go on at once.

Terry Lee, sitting on the white rail of the fence which ran around the tiny operations office, had his bad, stiff leg stretched out to the warmth of the sun. Terry Lee had been a pilot once, back in the days when Gates had knocked the gasps from the paying customers with wing walking and incredible stunting. And Terry Lee had kept going until the time, three years ago, when he had set his last plane to earth, a scrambled mess of junk. But it hadn't junked his hopes, and it hadn't kept him away from the flying game. For years he had built racers for his own contesting, and now, if he could build a pursuit plane faster than any other pursuit plane in the world . . .

Kip Lee was beside him, leaning against the fence, one battered boot crossing the other, a new helmet dangling and swinging from her small, capable hand. The sun made her silken yellow hair sparkle. Her big sky-blue eyes were sad.

"Aw, I won't let it get me down," she was saying. "But gosh, for years and years and years, ever since I used to sneak my pigtails down a block from home, I've carried Bill around in my head, in my baggage, in my ambitions. Why shouldn't I? You taught him to fly. You made him into about the hottest thing in the air. And that was my ambition. To get so good that he would pat me on the head and say, 'Fine!' Well—that's all over."

"Come off!" said Terry, her brother. "You *must* have looked funny, and, anyhow, you got your revenge—"

"Yeah? I land without my wheels. I couldn't get them down. And then he laughs at me like a baboon and tells everybody 'dames can't fly.' All these years, all I've lived for was to have him give me a big smile and say, 'Fine!' And he laughs at me! Why, I used to tag that idiot around like a pup, hanging on every word he said! And last night at the embassy he didn't even recognize me. Not even when I was introduced as 'Miss Lee'!"

Terry shrugged, but his eyes were sympathetic on his sister.

"You've changed a lot. You're a magazine cover now—and then you were just a gawky kid with pigtails. And freckles. How should *he* know?"

"Yeah? He's a swell-headed sap, that's what *he* is. I could kill him!"

"From your account of last night, you darn near did."

"Yeah."

23

She smiled a little, remembering how scared Bill had been, lifting her out of that ship. But still it was not revenge enough. To laugh at her and say dames couldn't fly and—"I hate him!" she cried suddenly, tears stinging her eyes.

Terry's oil-burned old face softened as he pulled her toward him. "Look, kid. Bill's all right—"

"Then why didn't he ever get in touch with you after you crashed?" she flared. "And here you are trying to put over the 41 and he's come up to test the only crate that can edge you out. Yeah, sure, he's all right—except that he doesn't know his own friends when the world begins to sing songs about *him*!"

"Sure. He's got a good job," said Terry, fishing for his pipe. "He rates a good job. What could *I* pay him? Besides, I haven't told him what I was doing. He doesn't know that Lee Aircraft and Terry Lee are one and the same."

"He's stupid if he doesn't guess!"

"Look, honey! Bill knew I crashed!"

"He did. Sure he did."

"He wired two thousand dollars to my hospital. And he's written me three or four letters since that have been forwarded to me. But until I can pay him back or offer him something—"

"Then he doesn't know?"

"No. And why should I tell him I'm shoestringing it here? I can't let him sink his last dime into such a place."

"But he's testing the one plane—"

"Yes. And if he found out he was competing against my ship, he'd quit, and then he would be out a lot of money. So he isn't going to know if you and I can help it. We'll make this 97 job strut its stuff, and we'll beat out BCA's 41. I can design 'em, and you can make 'em sing in the sky."

And then she remembered Bill standing there, laughing at her again. And she heard, once more, his remark to Cannard about "dames." And she suddenly jammed her helmet on her head and started toward Hangar Two, where an Airdevil Sportster sat.

"Whither bound?" said Terry.

"Any harm in going down and watch the 41's first tests?" Terry grinned.

"And I *still* think he's a conceited ape!" she flung back at him.

At noon a messenger found Bill sitting on a dolly under a No Smoking sign, lazily puffing upon a cigarette. Bill was outwardly his calm, indolent self, but inwardly he was still asking questions that went unanswered. *Irma* had little stability. *Irma* was the cousin of a truck, the sister of a banshee, and the daughter of ill-assorted crates. Why had she, at the very last instant, decided to fly herself? *Irma* certainly had never done it before.

"Mr. Cannard says he wants to see you, Mr. Trevillian. I guess you're going to start hopping 41, huh?"

"Yeah," said Bill. "Hey, Straud!"

Albert paused on *Irma*'s catwalk, a monkey wrench in his fist and grease upon his cheerful face. "Yeah?"

"You find anything wrong with the controls yet?" said Bill.

"Not a thing," said Albert.

"Huh," said Bill. And he got up to tag the messenger

toward a group of engineers and officials who were gathering for the slaughter.

"Is he goin' bugs?" said Greasy, taking a fresh chaw. "These controls are perfect, and yet he's got us going over 'em again and again, when we ought to be tuning up the crate for him."

"Yeah," said Albert.

BCA 41 was already on the line, 1,200 hp Allington engines muttering promises about what it was about to do to a couple of innocent clouds which drifted unconcerned in the deep blue of the sky.

"Are you all right, Bill?" said Cannard.

"Yeah," said Bill.

"Now look, Bill—we've got all the bugs we could think of out of 41. She's a sweeter ship than the other two we built of her type. She's fast and she's able, and she'll outfly—"

"Yeah," said Bill, "but maybe it'd be a good idea to let me find that out for myself."

"Sure, Bill. Hell, yes! Well, there she is. What're you going to do?"

Bill looked sleepily at the plane and then at the tense engineers. And the engineers looked at the plane and then at Bill. There was little love lost—there never is—between the swivel chair and the cockpit, where design was concerned. The engineers looked both anxious and jealous as Bill started to go over the plane as though somebody might have forgotten a ship needed wings.

BCA 41 was extraordinary in the lack of resemblance to the usual pursuit job. Instead of being a compact set of wings, fuselage and engine, streamlined to the *nth*, it was really two ships. Each of the two engines swept back into a tail, and the fuselage was just a Plexiglas bomb between the engines and the outriggers. The wings swooped sharply up at the ends, in an attempt to give her stability, and were hugely slotted, to cut her landing speed from the hundred and ten miles per hour it might have been to the sixty-five it had to be.

The pilot's cockpit was out in front, with visibility all around except back and down, but the gunner's cockpit, back to back with the pilot's, commanded this blind spot. The thing would mount eight machine guns in the wings and a motor cannon, 20 mm, firing through the hub of each prop, as well as a double Lewis firing straight aft.

The idea looked sound, for no other ship could get directly on its tail; and as, between them, pilot and observer could see all there was to see, it was doubtful if she could be suddenly attacked without warning. From a war pilot's viewpoint, she was all a plane should be. But just now the question was, could she stay all in one piece in the sky?

Bill looked into things and kicked things and shook his head as though very sad about the whole affair. The engineers jittered. Bill frowned and pursed his lips and thumped the wings. The engineers muttered. Bill listened to the idling Allingtons and sighed. The engineers appeared ready to take off themselves, ship or no ship.

Greasy and Albert Straud helped Bill into his chute. And then Albert pitched a hundred-and-fifty-pound sandbag up to a greaseball, who grunted and lowered it into the gunner's pit. Albert got up and lashed it down.

"Well," said Bill, "personally, I'll take vanilla."

The engineers frothed.

Bill slid into the forward seat and unlocked the controls. He wabbled them, looking around to see if all the flippers and rudders worked, and was apparently disappointed that they did. He revved the engines into a frightful din and watched the panel, with all its countless faces, for a story which also seemed to weary him. He slid open the hood again and beckoned urgently to the engineers, who instantly forged up against the blasting slipstream, ready with a thousand explanations as to why something wasn't working.

"Say!" shouted Bill against the yowling motors. "If Begging Baby wins the third at Bowie, will you radio it up to me?"

The engineers properly reduced to a gibbering frenzy, Bill took to the runway.

With haunted eyes Cannard watched him taxi BCA 41 up and down the field, testing out her horizontal control. This went on for fifteen or twenty minutes, while the dust from beside the concrete strips drifted higher and higher under the blast of the props. Bill would speed up and then slow. He would ground loop and come back again.

Finally he drifted to a stop before the group and beckoned up the mechanics.

"Left rudder feels slacker than the right," he said, standing on the catwalk and smoking a cigarette. The mechs promptly made the adjustment.

An Airdevil Sportster floated in for a landing and taxied out of the runway to the line. Bill climbed back into the pilot's seat and closed the hood.

Cannard again watched with twitching lips and dilated

eyes. Bill took the 41 to the east-west run and, kicking her into the wind, gave her full throttle. The blast was enough to blow down the hangars. The 41 leaped ahead so fast that it blurred. It lifted ten feet, and then the engines were cut and again its wheels touched. At the far end, Bill came to a braked stop. He taxied back to the group.

"Tab control seems stiff," he said, getting out for another smoke. "Ease it up, will you?"

The mechs eased it up, and once more Bill taxied out to the east-west run. And this time, when he javelined into the sky, he kept on going.

Quickly building a little altitude, he banked gently to the left and then to the right, but by that time he was out of sight.

"Gee!" said an awed voice at Cannard's right. "That thing sure travels!"

Cannard glanced aside and then away before he realized who it was. "Oh, hello, Miss Lee. Come to do a little spying, huh?"

"Yeah," said Kip Lee. "And I'm discouraged."

"Ha!" said Cannard, with no mirth whatever. "Where the hell has he gotten to?"

There was a rushing drone which swiftly became a bellow and Bill was over them and gone once more.

"Gosh," said Kip. "I'm not only discouraged, I'm groggy!"

"Ha!" said Cannard. "What the hell does he think he's doing—taking a sightseeing tour of Virginia?"

"That thing must make five hundred and fifty miles an hour," said Kip.

"Yes. Hey, Tom! Radio Bill to come back!"

But before Tom could contact the ship on his portable field set, Bill was overhead again. And even those in the crowd who knew little about the way planes should fly could see that something was wrong!

Bill tried to bank into the runway and then shot skyward again. He verticaled and once more attempted to shoot a landing. His wheels were down and his gun was cut, but again he failed. The 41 went racketing out of sight into the horizon haze and appeared once more, heading in downwind!

"He's crazy!" wailed Cannard.

Downwind! And his wing slots were apparently closed. He was doing a hundred and ten in the air with both guns cut and props nearly still, and the fifteen-mile breeze boosted it to a hundred and twenty-five ground speed! And the ship was not even headed for the runway, but for the rough strips in between!

Kip's fingers sank into Cannard's arm and Cannard didn't feel it. Nobody breathed. The plane wasn't going to make another try. This would be *it*!

The engine of the crash wagon started. Hot papas got into their helmets and girded themselves to haul a fried pilot from a blazing wreck. Some people were already running forward; others were frozen to the earth.

Downwind at a hundred and twenty-five! And he was leveling off for a landing with half the field used up already—leveling off a full fifteen feet above the ground. The plane came down to stalling. It floated, devouring landing way at a terrific clip, seemingly eager to get at the high-tension lines and the fences which waited at the far end.

Abruptly plane and shadow met. The ship bounced and was forced back to earth. Again it bounced and came down on its tail wheels, hitting its gear and tipping up until it was impossible for the props not to clip earth. With two sharp *pings* they did. Then all wheels were down, and the fences and wires were only feet away. The plane ground looped, rocking up to knock an aileron against the dust. It settled back and coasted slowly. It was trembling like a horse that has missed a hurdle. . . .

Kip began to breathe again. She felt too weak to run, but she found herself running. She felt dizzy and ill, and at the same time glad.

She grabbed the tail of the crash wagon as it shot by and clung on until it skidded to a halt beside the battered plane. She leaped down and was up on the catwalk, tearing at the hood, before any other had begun to approach it afoot.

And then Kip stopped. She had the hood open and a string of profanity came smoking forth. And Kip began to grin.

Bill was a wreck. The oil line to the gauge had parted company, nearly drowning him in a bath of hot oil. He was black—all black. When his streaming hands reached up to shove away his goggles, his eyes, surrounded by two white rings, glared forth.

He saw Kip. She had thrust her helmet into her pocket and the sun was in her yellow hair and her big sky-blue eyes were gleaming with glee.

Bill was shocked down to the darkest recesses of his soul. Suddenly he saw it all. This was the one who had landed

31

on the field. And the girl at the embassy. And the frozen controls—*Irma*—

Bill grew angrier and madder and angrier.

And Kip laughed. With one wild yelp of mirth which could no longer be held in check, she laughed. And she kept on laughing.

"Dames—" she sputtered. "Dames can't—*fly!*"

Bill tried to mop away the oil. He climbed out on the catwalk with every intention of throttling her. And she nearly fell off the leading edge.

"Dames—dames—" wept Kip, "can't *fly!*"

Then some kind soul averted murder by pulling Bill toward the ambulance. . . .

On the following day, Greasy Hannagan, wandering into the third hangar, was startled by a pair of boots sticking out, feet up, from the pilot's seat of the BCA 41. The boots were battered, but obviously from the best Italian shop. There was only one pair of boots like that anywhere about the field, and as that pair belonged to Bill Trevillian, Greasy came to the brilliant conclusion that Bill's feet must be in the boots and that, therefore, Bill was upside down in the BCA 41 third ship. Yes—from the occasional mutters of profanity, it was Bill. Had to be Bill.

Greasy took a chaw and sat down on the wing. After a little, Bill came struggling forth. There was a long lot of him to extricate from that position and it took some time. But finally there was Bill, upright again. In his hand he held a gauge which he had pulled from the back of the panel. On his face was an angry cloud.

"I got it," said Bill.

"What?" said Greasy.

"The oil pressure gauge. On the ship I nearly smashed yesterday, there was nothing whatever wrong with the panel. I have the photographs of the readings from the automatic camera, and I can't see a trace of warning for the breaking of that oil line."

"Well?" said Greasy. "A faulty line, that's all."

"Yeah? Well, it *isn't* all! This gauge here has been opened since it was installed. The little clips here show abrasions made after the instrument company gave it the final coat of paint."

"I don't get it," said Greasy, frowning.

"It's open and shut," said Bill. "And right now I am making sure."

He took the air hose off the paint sprayer and, with reducers, made it fast to the back of the gauge. There was already one gauge on the air hose, an accurate one, tested every week. Bill shot on the air. The gauge in his hand, which he had taken from the third BCA 41, registered a pressure of sixty pounds. The air gauge contradicted it to the extent of thirty pounds, for it registered *ninety*.

"There!" said Bill.

"I still don't get it!" said Greasy.

"Look," said Bill. "This oil gauge is set to register far less pressure than is actually in the lines. That means that the oil pumps are set way up and it won't show on this gauge. Now do you see?"

"Nope," said Greasy.

"Listen, dummy! If a pilot sees his oil pressure going up, he revs down. If the oil pressure goes up and he doesn't rev down he either breaks his line or spoils his engines. The chances are that the line will break as it comes into the panel, or that the face of the gauge itself will go blooie. In either case it is certain that the lines will break under enough pressure. And either the pilot is blinded or the hot oil catches fire. *Now* do you get it?"

"Gee!" said Greasy.

"So that crash yesterday was all laid out for me in advance!"

"Gosh, who'd do a thing like that?" said Greasy, blinking.

"I'll tell you who. The only rival BCA 41 has is the L97."

"Aw, naw!" said Greasy.

"Aw, yes!" snarled Bill. "Maybe it was a setup for a gag, and maybe it was with malice aforethought to sabotage this ship and put over the L97. But that Lee kid is behind it!"

"Aw, hell!" said Greasy. "You're off your crankshaft! Miss Lee is a good scout. She's aces. She wouldn't—"

"Yeah? Well, when a ten-million-dollar contract is at stake, people will do anything."

"You're just all het up because she laughed at you," said Greasy. "Well, hell, Bill, you laughed at her first!"

"I didn't try to wreck her ship first."

"Aw, look, Bill, Miss Lee—"

"Where are they building the L97?"

"Calver, Maryland. But look here, Bill, you better not—"

34

"A ten-million-dollar contract," said Bill, "is enough to make anybody do anything. I was wrong about her. I thought she was swell down at the embassy and I was willing to lay down my life—"

"You met her someplace else?"

"Yeah. In Washington, worse luck."

"Oh, so it was Miss Lee that was out here flying with you night before last. News, you know, gets around."

"So what?"

"I don't know who it was. The hangar man said she was with you and came back to get an evening bag that she left in your ship—"

"What's that? She came back *here?*"

"Sure. You go past this place to get to Calver, and she drove in and asked to get her evening bag. The hangar man—"

"So! She came back!"

Bill was already on the phone, dragging the night hangar man out of a well-earned sleep. "Look," said Bill, forgetting that that is hard to do through a phone, "this is Bill Trevillian. The other night I came out here with a girl and I hear she stopped back to get her evening bag. Clean the cumulus out of your wits and remember. How long did she talk to you?"

The hangar man mumbled, "Oh, about half an hour I guess. She sure knew her planes."

Bill hung up. "So! She talked to the hangar man for half an hour. A good mech, working fast, could jim that pressure gauge in that time and set up the oil pumps. She came in here and covered—"

"Aw, you're loopy!" said Greasy. "Miss Lee—"

35

"Ten million bucks and a laugh!" said Bill, now white-hot. And he flung himself out the door and into Greasy's roadster and went streaking past the startled noses of transport planes. His tires screamed as he careened out into the highway, Calver-bound.

"He who laughs last laughs and laughs!" snarled Bill.

Back at the hangar, Albert Straud drifted up. "What's wrong with Trevillian?"

"Aw, he's in a spin. Look, Albert, get a gauge—this one's been monkeyed with—and install it in the third ship there, will you?"

Albert looked up at the gauge and then at the plane. It was nearly noon, but he worked calmly. When the whistle blew he went with the others out through the gate. According to his watch he had two minutes and a half to make a contact.

"Sure is hot, ain't it?" said the clerk.

"Yeah, sure is," said Albert, slipping into the booth. "Get me Calver—" And then, "Hello, John, this is George."

"Hello, George." And he could not resist adding, "I hear you had a little trouble with this and that yesterday."

"Shut up! Trevillian is on his way to the Lee plant. You'll spot him because he's lanky and sleepy-looking, and maybe you've seen his pictures. He found the altered gauge on the third ship and he's laying the blame on Lee Aircraft—"

"Good. L97 goes up for altitude this afternoon. A lot of officers here. There's enough altocirrus for ice, and the de-icers are short-circuited."

"We've got something going," said Albert. And, hearing

someone enter the next booth, "Well, John, I hope you make the grade all right. I gotta eat. S'long."

"I'll make the grade," said John. "'Bye."

There were a lot of officers at the Lee plant, and the fence which ran about the tiny operations office looked as if it had been decorated with all the braid in existence. French and British aeronautical experts chatted together in low voices, from time to time hopefully glancing toward the line, where three mechs were giving the L97 its final check. Terry Lee hobbled among them answering questions and beaming, nearly bursting with pride at the thought of what his precious baby, the L97, was about to show them.

Kip, in white boots and breeches and shirt, had drawn all the junior officers into her vicinity and they nearly shattered themselves each time she indicated that she needed a cigarette.

"Well, Lee, old chap," said a British colonel, "if it does all you say it will do—and don't think we aren't hoping it will—why, there will be a lot of changes around here, eh?" And he waved his seat-stick in the direction of the weed-grown field and the sagging old hangar and machine shop which had gone six years without a coat of paint. "But what I can't understand is how you've managed to research and build the two ships you have built."

"I researched 'em in the sky," said Terry. "And I pawned my grandmother's false teeth. I've wanted to build this plane for years, but it hasn't been more than six months since they finally got out a twenty-four-hundred-horse engine. That was all she needed."

"I say, aren't you a bit squeamish about letting your sister fly it, though? It's an X job—"

"Kip?" said Terry with a laugh. "Why, Kip cut her first teeth on a rip cord ring, and that's a fact. She was flying in planes before she could walk. They don't come better than Kip."

"Yes. Yes, of course. I know she's won races and stunting exhibitions and all that, and I'm not questioning either her reputation or her ability. But it is, may I say, a rather dangerous thing kicking a killer like that around the sky."

"Never mind," said Terry. "I built it and I know it's right. And she saw it built and knows every bolt in it."

The colonel looked at Kip—who could barely be seen inside the ring of junior officers—and shook his head in wonder. A slight little girl like that and a ship which might make five hundred and seventy-five miles an hour—! Strange people, these Americans.

A battered roadster braked to a screeching halt and out of the dust stalked Bill Trevillian.

Two officers recognized him instantly and spoke to him, but Bill went right on by, too mad to see anyone but Kip.

With all the junior officers helping, she had gotten into her parachute harness and was being lifted up to the pit. By the time Bill arrived, she had pulled on her helmet and buckled her belt and the junior officers were all backing up to avoid the slipstream of the gigantic prop. She looked like a little doll put down in the midst of gleaming, lethal machinery to be torn to bits, but the picture had no meaning for Bill. She was jabbing at the throttles when he vaulted up to the wing and yanked back the hood.

"Hello," said Kip. "What's the idea?"

"You know what the idea is," said Bill. "I found that gauge one of your pals jimmied up!"

"Huh? Say, you've sprung your prop! What do you mean, 'gauge that one of my pals jimmied up'?"

"Sure, act innocent!" said Bill. "It was a good joke—only it might have killed me!"

"Mister Trevillian," said Kip, "if you don't get off that wing and stop talking blather—"

"Sure! Pretend you didn't fix that gauge so I'd get oil in my puss! Sure! Pretend you aren't doing your bit to help your company get the contract away from BCA. *Yeah!*"

And now she was mad. She was as white as her shirt. "Why, you thick-skulled—" And she blotted it out by jamming the throttle into the board. The blast from twenty-four hundred horses was enough to tear a man in half and Bill hadn't had any too good a grip on the hood. He was bowled off the wing like a rag in a hurricane. And then the junior officers had him.

Kip closed the hood with a bang and, without so much as a wave at the spectators, shot the big pursuit off toward the runway.

Terry Lee limped forward and rescued Bill. But Bill was still too angry to see or think about anything but Kip, and he was led all the way back to the fence before he realized that the voice on his right was very familiar. He turned with annoyance and then, suddenly, recognized Terry Lee.

"Thought you'd get around to it by and by," said Terry. "How you been?"

He was bowled off the wing like a rag in a hurricane.

Bill looked at Terry and then at the stiff leg. "Why—I thought you were still flying someplace. What's the matter with you?"

"They say," said Terry, "that me'n planes are through so far as the sky is concerned. I'm building them."

"You . . . you're Lee Aircraft—! Good lord," cried Bill, "I never connected them up . . . never once!"

"Well, there are plenty of Lees in this world."

"But you—then you're the one that's building the L97—that L stands for Lee!"

"Yep."

"And then—then Miss Lee is *Kip* Lee!"

"Sure."

Bill's face was scarlet.

"Oh, my God! Say, I'm in a spin—a flat spin! Oh, lord, have I made a fool of myself! Why doesn't somebody tell me these things? Kip! Why, I haven't seen her since she used to steal my tools to build dollhouses. What a change!"

"Yeah, isn't it," said Terry. "You know, her one ambition has always been to get as good as you are, Bill. She's got every newspaper picture of you that was ever published. And she's damn near made good her brag."

"Oh, I'm a split-tailed jackass!" said Bill. "Terry, you've got to square this. You know what I just did? I accused her of fixing my oil pressure gauge. It caused my crash yesterday, and I thought, because I laughed at her, she pulled a gag or was trying to sabotage BCA or— My God, Terry, you've got to square this! Kip, little old Kip—"

"There she goes!" cried several in the crowd.

Everyone, down to the field cat, was watching the L97.

The ship was something to look at, too, for it accelerated so fast on the takeoff that eyes had to jump ahead of it to see it at all.

It was of a different design from the BCA 41, in that it followed a more conventional pattern, having but one tail and one engine. It covered its blind spot behind by having its gunner's pit nearly up against its rudder and gun mountings so fixed that a gunner there could cover all but the smallest possible area below. It would carry ten machine guns and one rapid-firing motor cannon placed through its crankshaft. It saved the weight of duplicated fuel lines and cylinders required for two engines, and for that reason could probably cover more air faster than the BCA. And that gigantic engine was hauling it aloft now at the climbing rate of a thousand feet in ten seconds, a black bullet fired straight up.

"I say!" said the colonel, blinking into the sun. "That thing can't be fully equipped and fully loaded!"

"With guns, ammunition and gas," Terry assured him. "Just as if it was going up there to shoot down a Dornier."

The point caught the colonel's fancy and he smiled a pleased smile.

But Kip wasn't smiling. Her face was stony and her knuckles on the stick were dead white. The jets of white flame from the exhausts were as nothing compared to the jets which stabbed from her eyes.

Saboteur, indeed! The big baboon! To accuse her, Kip Lee, the kid who had idolized him, of sabotaging his lousy ship—! And straight up went the L97, straight up at the altocirrus which spread a lacy, delicate pattern seven miles above the earth.

Behind her the field fell away with such shrinking rapidity that people became dots and then barns became dots, and finally fields became dots. The murky horizon stretched further and further until, ever so slightly, the curvature of the earth became apparent.

She jabbed an oxygen tube into her mouth and turned on her heat, for it was getting colder as she streaked up, and at four miles a man finds it impossible to breathe.

The superchargers in the giant engine were whining shrilly and the automatically pitched prop twisted as it tried to get a bigger bite out of rarer air. The plane was all power and flash and sound, and now, at twenty-five thousand, it was still going up at the rate of twenty seconds per thousand feet. Fastened against the panel before her were the sealed barographs the French and British had had installed, for they trusted no instruments but their own. And by this time the plane was wholly invisible in the sky, except to powerful glasses.

The stratosphere pursuit showed no sign of wanting to quit at thirty thousand. Kip, still mad, automatically checked over her instruments and automatically registered the tale of every flickering needle. All was well.

Thirty-one thousand, and the first wisps of cirrus, featherlike strata of ice crystals, were shredded by the wings. Kip switched on the de-icers.

Thirty-two, thirty-three, thirty-four, thirty-five— The earth seemed milky, seen through the sheets of clouds, and the horizon was too thick to be visible.

Thirty-six, thirty-seven—

Ever so little, the ship began to complain about it. The

43

engine heat started down slowly. The controls were a little sloppy. Kip sat forward and leveled out. She'd let this demon take a breather and then try to push it another thousand or two. Her eyes wandered to the earth below, but the earth was only partly visible, a detached and unimportant thing which one found with surprise.

At a lessened climbing angle, she again nursed the plane higher. Thirty-eight, thirty-nine— It was trembling, seemingly ready to stall. The controls were wabbly—

Too wabbly! And then too stiff!

Kip forgot her anger in that second. She saw the right aileron bent down and could not bring it up. It was caught! *Ice!* The whole leading edge of the wing was thick with frost! And ice had gotten into the hinge of the aileron.

The ship twisted slowly over on its side and then, with a suddenness which left her heart a thousand feet above, curved like a slashing sword and, nose at earth, engine screaming as it revved, headed down!

It was a tight spiral which gradually wound into itself. Kip worked at the aileron with the stick, trying to ease it loose. The earth had turned into a kid's top and all the colors blurred into a monotone, so fast was it going round. She cut her gun, but this plane was more a bullet than a well-behaved ship and the speed indicator was already getting up toward terminal velocity—and keeping on upward. Six hundred, six-fifty, seven hundred, seven—she was going at the speed of sound! Going straight down, and she'd crash before the passage of her plane was heard. She'd dig even before the scream of her wretchedly protesting wings told of her plight!

She coolly worked at the aileron. It was warmer in these lower strats, but not warm enough to melt that ice. And as she went she picked up a heavier and heavier layer of white death.

Twenty-six thousand, twenty-five, twenty-four, twenty-three—

Around and around, like the blade of an electric mixer. There was still a chance. But she knew better than to try to bail out at this speed, for the air out there would be like ten hurricanes added into their total speeds and her head would be snapped and her back broken before she could ever get free.

She looked at her ammeters and noted that they were registering no current drag. Somewhere, probably in the de-icers, wires had burned through. She had failed in one respect. She had not noticed those ammeters in time to know that her de-icers were not functioning.

Nineteen, eighteen, seventeen thousand feet. Still three and a half miles high and going earthward at six hundred feet a second. In less than a minute—

She hauled back on the stick with all her strength and her arms were almost yanked from their sockets as the plane began to flatten its spiral into a spin. The ASI went mad now, for it could not register speed with the tail flying about in a wider arc than the motor. She brought the thing up to a stall and then let it fall out. Again she flattened the spiral into a spin and whipstalled out of that. Anything for a little delay. And it came to her, as the blood rushed downward from her head with each attempt, that this plane wouldn't need any gravity tests if it withstood this—for the maneuver was one to wrench out any bolt that could be wrenched.

45

Delay—delay! Just a few seconds, here at eight thousand feet, and that aileron might let go. Whipstall, spiral, spin. She was getting dazed with the beating she was taking, for she was being buffeted all about, and even with the long practice she had had, she could not fight off dizziness forever.

Whipstall with a vicious swoop and into a giddy spiral. Flatten the spin, stand her up on the nose, swoop off and into another spiral. And each time she fought to get the aileron free.

She wondered what they were thinking about all this on the ground. She really ought to make a note, in case she didn't survive it. Then Terry would know that something had to be done about the de-icers—

With a jolt that sent the ship hurtling into a reverse snap roll, the aileron gave way. With the speed of instinct she brought the plane level and cut in the engine. The Allington sputtered coldly after its long idling, but it took hold and she went rocketing across the fields, looking for the port.

Somehow she eased into position and lowered her wheels. Somehow she floated to a stall and touched three points at once. Somehow she kicked rudder and got the plane to the line. And then she fainted.

Bill, losing his languor, pushed some junior officers in the face with his right boot and yanked open the hood. Anxiously he lifted Kip's head. She had bitten the oxygen tube mouthpiece all the way through, and now it fell from her lips. Bill pulled up her goggles.

Sleepily she came to and saw him. A smile crept over her face and dreamily she said, "Oh, Bill—"

"You're okay, Kip. Altitude silly, that's all. And gosh, I'm sorry! How was I to know you were Kip? Gee, I feel so bad about it I—"

It was like sticking a pin into a black panther. The whole memory of it came back to her and again his angry accusation was ringing in her head.

"*So!*" cried Kip, throwing off her belt and standing up so suddenly that she almost knocked him down. "So I sabotaged your plane, did I? Well, how about *my* plane? How about my de-icers? Yes—how about them? Just because you thought in that evil, crawling mind of yours that I had something to do with your rotten flying, did that give you the right to short-circuit my de-icers? Get out of here! Get out of my sight before—before I turn these machine guns on you!"

The junior officers again hauled Bill down and hurried him to his car, no matter how he struggled.

"And *stay* out!" Kip shouted after him.

And then she sank down into the pilot's seat again, and despite all the praise she was getting and all the bravos about the plane—for they had not seen her come down at all—she held her face in her hands and wept big, bitter tears.

The BCA 41 streaked across the field. It verticaled, five miles away and back again, before a spectator could take a breath. Abruptly it snap rolled and went from that into a straight climb, and when it fell out of that it did an inverted falling leaf for three wriggles. It was a bullet that was being fired from all directions, and trying to track it by its sound would

47

have driven a man mad; for very often it was there almost as soon as its own sound was, and very often it was there and some other place before anyone could see that it had been anywhere in the first place.

"What the hell is the matter with him?" said Cannard. "Here! There! Up! Down! On his back and his belly, and picking daisies with his wings one minute and clouds the next. I'm tired of looking at the damned fool!"

Greasy spat philosophically. "Well, if you asked me, I'd say he was trying to work off the williewoofs."

"The what?"

"The whizzlejits."

"You mean he's mad?"

"I mean he's revved up till his mount bolts is coming loose. He's been like that all week. Ain't you seen it?"

Cannard was getting dizzy jerking his head to the left and right following the silver flashes. He turned his back on it, lit a cigarette and then threw it away. He swung some keys around and around on a silver chain and then jingled some pennies and nickels in his pocket.

"He did his tests all right for the British. Came through fine," said Cannard at last. "If the finals go all right, he'll get ten thousand bonus. So why the hell has he got the whizzlewoofs or whatever you said?"

"Girl trouble."

"Who? Bill Trevillian? Nuts, my friend. Not Bill Trevillian!"

"Yep," said Greasy, renewing his chaw. "'S'fac'. And she don't like him."

"Not like Bill? Say, that girl needs talking to—she must be crazy!" He dug the engine snarl out of his right ear and glanced with a wince at the BCA 41, which had just made the wind tee spin on the Operations office roof.

"Yep," said Greasy. "She's crazy. He came back here day before yesterday with a black eye. Not much of an eye, but it was black all right for a while."

"Black eye! You mean she slugged him?"

"Wouldn't be surprised. Maybe threw a wrench at him."

"A wrench! Say, look here, Greasy Hannagan—"

"I said a wrench."

"Who the devil—?"

"Kip Lee."

"*Who?*"

"'S'fac'," said Greasy. "Dunno what the trouble was exactly, but he got the idea she monkeyed up his crate and went roaring over full gun to zoom the place. I told him he was yelling up the wrong tree."

"Monkeyed up his plane? Say, am I in charge of this place or have I got BO? You mean to say somebody—"

"Yeah. Fixed a pressure gauge and the oil pumps. That was what caused his first crash—or almost caused it. And he said—"

"Kip Lee wouldn't do a thing like that. Nor Terry Lee either. Are you sure the gauge—"

"I saw it tested with my own eyes," said Greasy.

"Uh-*huh*!" said Cannard. "Anything else happen?"

"Not to Bill. Ever since that happened, he damn near takes the plane apart every morning—whichever one of 'em he's going to test. He found two nuts almost filed through on a strut yesterday, and a pin gone out of one wheel the day before—"

"You mean he's testing in the full knowledge that somebody is trying to wreck him? And you haven't told me about it? Why, by the wheels of hades, I ought to fire you on the spot! Sabotage in BCA!"

"Well—there are an awful lot of things that can get wrong with a plane. Bill said just lay low. If we talked about it, why, whoever it was would get scared. Bill said if he caught the guy red-handed, then he could maybe trace back and find out who it was that short-circuited the de-icers on the L97 and so prove to Kip Lee that he didn't do it because he thought she did things to his pressure gauge—"

"Oh! So we got romance in our business! So agents are trying to sabotage us and we can't keep an eye out because it might stop one of Cupid's arrows! Dispatcher! Bring that crazy whizzlewoof of a pilot down here and damned fast!"

Bill, radioed down and flagged down, finally did come down. And when he had eased his long body down the wing to concrete, he looked at Cannard and then Greasy and knew what was going on.

"Just had to talk, didn't you?" drawled Bill.

"Aw, he wanted to know why you was acting so crazy up there and so I told him. There ain't no harm in it. We won't catch the guy ourselves. Honest-to-Pete, Bill, I'm so stiff from sleeping in those 41s that I feel like I'd been eatin' plaster of Paris."

"My old pal Greasy!" said Bill, lighting a smoke and leaning against the 41.

"I ought to fire you both!" said Cannard. "Now give me all the details. Why, this afternoon, this very afternoon, the officers are coming out here to make the final comparisons between the two planes, and if that thing was to crash right in front of them they'd give Lee the contract so quick it'd scorch the paper! That ship you are flying seems to be holding together, but I'm going to have it checked part by part, bolt by bolt, rivet by rivet—"

"And rev by rev," said Bill. "But I've already checked it. You think I'd risk my neck in something I hadn't? That plane is all right, and it so happens that I'll drill the first gent that touches so much as one wire on it."

"Not even a refueling crew?"

"I'll do the refueling—and I'll do it out of sealed cans," drawled Bill.

"Why, this is a helluva note! You won't even trust my own workmen, and yet you won't tell me—"

"You open up about this and get the FBI crawling all over here and scare that gent away," said Bill, "and I'll feed you to the first prop I see!"

"But why—?"

"Because that's the way it is, that's all."

"Listen, Bill Trevillian! Just because you and Kip Lee have to get into a scrap about de-icers is no reason you can tell me how to run my own plant! I'm calling the FBI—right now, if not sooner!"

Cannard went away from there and Bill looked sleepily at Greasy. "Just Walter Winchell himself, aren't you?"

"Well," said Greasy, shifting uncomfortably, "I gotta think about your neck if you won't. Besides, we've got one FBI man here all the time, so what difference does another half-dozen make?"

"Cannard is a smart guy," said Bill. "He'll howl and rave about this sabotage until the roof comes off, and those French and British officers will just take it as an advance alibi in case BCA 41 falls apart. And if it does fall apart, then they'll *know* it was an alibi. I shoulda told Cannard that."

"You shoulda done a lot of things," said Greasy, "including stayin' away from Lee Aircraft that day."

"Greasy, just for that you can go get me a ham sandwich and a Coke. I gotta fortify myself against the invasion of Uncle Sam's bloodhounds."

Greasy was glad to oblige and went across the tarmac like a duck trying to get off the water. Bill stood and communed with his soul, idly snapping and unsnapping his goggles from his helmet.

A nondescript piece of humanity in overalls of the kind one takes for granted slouched up. "Telephone for you, Mr. Trevillian."

"Huh? Any idea who from?"

"Sounded like a lady, Mr. Trevillian. Long distance."

"Long—gosh!" And Bill went away from there in a rush. He picked up the down receiver of the hangar phone and told the mouthpiece hello, but the operator parroted, "Number, please."

"I had a call on this wire," said Bill.

"Sorry. The party must have hung up."

"Get me Calver. Get me Lee Aircraft in Calver!"

"Just a moment, please."

When the call got through to Lee Aircraft, Bill excitedly asked for Kip and waited with eagerness.

"Hello," said Kip.

"Hello. Look, this is Bill Trevillian. Did you call me just now?"

"Call *you*?" she said with scorn. "I should say not!" But she didn't hang up as swiftly as her voice would seem to indicate.

"Somebody said I had a call from a lady, long distance, and gee, I was hoping—"

"Probably somebody you jilted, Casanova!"

"No, look! You're coming over here this afternoon to test beside BCA 41. Look, I feel lousy about having to fly the ship that may take the contract—"

"Ha! So you're already grabbing for it, are you? So you're all set, are you? There's two planes in that exhibition, Bill Trevillian. And don't forget it."

"I didn't mean—"

"Tell it to whoever phoned you!" And she hung up.

Bill frowned in thought and reluctantly put the receiver back. When he was again beside his plane, the mech was nowhere to be seen and he couldn't remember which one it had been. There was no one else in sight and so he sat on the wing and waited for his sandwich and Coke.

A few minutes later Cannard came steaming up with a crew in tow.

"Now," he said energetically, "we're going to go over this ship bolt by bolt, rivet by rivet—"

"Yeah?" said Bill. "And have one of those monkeys pull out a cotter key someplace? Nope. This thing flies as is."

"Now, Bill—"

"That's the way it's got to be or I quit on the spot!"

Cannard studied him and finally decided that he meant it. He wandered away, dispersing the crew, leaving Bill in grim possession of the lists.

At two o'clock that afternoon the L97 landed at the BCA port and was immediately mobbed by the junior officers. Kip Lee, once more all in white, smiled sweetly upon all of them as she walked toward the stand from which the final contest would be observed. The gallant French would gladly have let her make her way across their bowed heads, and the pink-cheeked subalterns forgot all about the ladies who sighed for them in England. Only once did Kip's smile leave her and that was when she saw Bill. She passed by him and he was right royally snubbed.

Cannard and Terry Lee were waiting at the foot of the steps with a British colonel, and when the two pilots stood before them, the colonel said, "This is the last proof we must have, you know. We are already quite pleased with the performance of both these American planes. But the question which we must prove is whether one can outmaneuver the other. The camera guns which have been installed upon your wings and mounted in the after pits are connected to the Bowden trips in your cockpits and aligned with your ring sights. Of course the chap who gets the most hits is not necessarily flying the best plane, but I think we can tell which one is top hole by the results. Now, are there any questions?"

"Yes," said Kip.

"Very well. What is the question?"

"Why can't we use live ammunition?"

The colonel was quite puzzled, but the mechanics and engineers about, who were in the know, guffawed, puzzling the colonel even further.

Kip turned on her heel and walked to her plane. The junior officers put her into her parachute and then lifted her up. An English boy, swaggering with the honor, climbed into the L97's gunner's pit and settled his helmet with a flourish, scowling the while at the BCA 41.

Greasy helped Bill up and then climbed up himself, hauling a filthy helmet down over his ears. Greasy took a fresh chaw and gazed contemptuously at the English lad.

"May the best ship win!" said the colonel, above the mutter of engines.

Kip glowered down the line at the BCA 41 and then shot the throttle forward to send the big pursuit leaping straight out across the field. She was paying no attention to either wind or runway, taking the air in so short a distance that she seemed to need no run at all. She snapped the wing slots closed as soon as she was a hundred feet from the earth and the effect was that of spurs into the flanks of a bronc. Very swiftly she trimmed with the tabs to stabilize for the weight of the young English gunner, and then, climbing in a wide turn, looked back to find that Bill had followed almost upon her tail.

"Showoff!" she growled. And immediately banked the other way to corkscrew skyward and away from him with such speed that between tick-ticks of the heart five miles separated them.

Bill was also climbing, keeping her in sight. The way she had glared at him and then snubbed him had burned like hot iron into his emotions and he was in a state of mind to put her in her place, Terry Lee or no Terry Lee. Snub him, accuse him of sabotage, refuse to see him, laugh at him—! *Arrrrr!* Wait until he got the camera on her!

Greasy peered speculatively at the black plane and spat indifferently into the slipstream aft. He leaned upon the camera gun and sent an unheard song of considerable bawdy content outward with the racket of the two engines. Some of Bill's mood entered into him. Far below he could see the bright spots of color which marked the stand, but as these were already fading to a dot he soon lost interest. Kip's black ship was clawing for height, determined to get the better of the first contact through additional altitude.

But each time Kip jacked her altimeter another notch, so did Bill, and as they were climbing, one left and one right, they were now a thousand yards, now five miles apart and barely able to keep each other in sight. Kip slipped her oxygen mask into place and the English boy did the same, for they were now getting up to sixteen thousand feet.

Bill stood the BCA 41 on its nose and scrambled for the large white globes of altocumulus which drifted like loose wads of cotton at twenty-one thousand feet. He went through a hole and, for six hundred feet of height, lost Kip. But when he burst through into the achingly blue sky and scanned the fantastic land of cloud mountains and snowy castles, he felt rather than heard additional din about him and quickly shied away. He had not and could not then see the other plane, so swiftly had it dived upon him and beyond him. He glanced at Greasy and was startled to find that Greasy was swinging the camera gun back into position, holding up one finger to Bill.

Bill climbed with everything he had, staring around to locate the black ship. He caught a glimpse of it nearly a mile away and coming back at a little less than six hundred miles an hour. In one second it was almost crashing into him. In another it was a mile beyond.

Then it was Bill's turn, for he had it in sight. Full gun he swooped around and down upon it and the gap closed by half while Kip sought to loop, snap roll and return, not realizing that he was with her. He looped tightly almost the same instant that she did, and when the cloud world had finished turning over he had only to bank and center her rudder in his sights. She was not there long, hardly more than three seconds, and then, before he could trace her, she was gone again.

For nearly eight seconds he searched for her in vain, without realizing that Greasy was bawling at him with all his lungs. Bill looked back and found the nose of the black ship nearly between the twin tails of the BCA 41. He slipped. Kip slipped with him. He dived, she dived. He went into a loop, reversed. The black ship was still there, as though a picture stuck on the back plates of the Plexiglas.

Then Bill became diabolical. He cut the 41's throttle with a sudden yank and shot it on instantly. But that brief falter was enough to make Kip shoot upward and past to avoid collision with him.

And now he had the black plane centered in his sights and was conscious of the English lad up there, pink cheek to ring mount, clicking merrily away, and every shot a perfect score. Bill became clever again. He swooped a little and was in the one blind spot of the 97, making his camera click with all possible speed. And then he was clicking empty space, and looking swiftly all around, he could nowhere see the black plane.

Greasy was pointing way out toward the cloud horizon. Bill finally picked it up, though they were some four miles apart. The two ships decided to contact on the same instant and two seconds later passed so close together that he saw Kip's set face as clearly as though he had really had time to look at it. He decided it must have been an illusion. You can't see anything when the combined speed is around eleven hundred miles an hour, any more than you can stand and watch a .22 bullet go by—for it travels at much the same speed.

They lost each other again, and for a long time, fifteen or twenty seconds, each patrolled in vain.

Then Kip saw a flash of silver and instantly dived at it across ten miles of sky and passed, with only two clicks of her camera gun to show for it. She felt she was doing badly. Their shots had nearly balanced so far, as nearly as she could tell, except for the moment when Bill had been back and below. Then he had gotten several, all perfect hits, from his after gun.

She looped and came hurtling back for another, better

shot. And, strangely enough, she got a perfect one. Either Bill did not see her as she went past or he had gone to sleep, for she was able to loop a second time and come up from below for three direct hits. She went over the hump at the top and again scored.

Was something wrong? This, she told herself, was taking candy from kids! She flashed around, turning through a three-mile arc, and got on the silver ship's tail for even further scores. And Bill was making no effort at all to avoid her. In fact he didn't seem to be making any effort to fly. And where was Greasy? The gunner's camera had its nose pointed skyward! And no face behind the ring—!

Bill searched the limitless expanse of white and blue for a trace of the black plane and searched in vain, for its wings, unfortunately for him, were dull and showed no tendency to give themselves away by flashing.

Greasy searched as well, for he was getting excited about this and felt he hadn't had a proper chance to roll up a decent score.

Greasy stood with camera grips clenched, chewing very fast and staring everywhere. And then something hard was jammed into his spine. Greasy whirled. Had Bill suddenly gone loco—?

But it wasn't Bill behind him. It was Albert Straud. And Bill was facing the other way, forward, watching the sky in that direction for some quick sign of Kip.

Greasy blinked, wondering for a moment whether Albert Straud was a ghost. But then he saw that the small bomb bay which lay between the two seats and was intended to hold small bombs for trench strafing was open and empty of bombs. Albert Straud had been there when they had taken off. He certainly was no ghost! Greasy took heart.

"Can it!" said Greasy. "This is no time—"

It was nearly impossible to hear above the engines unless a man shouted—and Albert Straud quickly jabbed most of the breath from Greasy.

Placing his mouth close to Greasy's ear, Albert Straud yelled, "Open your port and bail out!"

"You're nuts!" shouted Greasy. "Put that gun away and—"

"Bail out or I'll fire!"

"Aw, Albert! What the hell—"

"The name is von Straub. Erich von Straub, colonel of the German air force. Bail out or I'll kill you!"

Greasy tried to grab the gun, but von Straub countered with a stunning blow to the side of Greasy's head. Greasy slumped, and von Straub swiftly pried open the port and heaved Greasy out. The mech was a dwindling dot far behind, already falling.

Displaying no emotion about it and without even wondering whether or not Greasy would come around enough to yank his rip cord, von Straub climbed over the bomb bay from which he had emerged and, with as little feeling as he had shown with Greasy, brought the butt of the automatic down upon Bill's skull.

Bill sagged, reaching instinctively for the switches to cut them, but failing in the effort. As the ship began to fall off on one wing, von Straub quickly hauled Bill to one side and, reaching over, steadied the ship while he crawled into Bill's place. Once there, he made an effort to thrust Bill out through the hood, but he could not manage it and fly, for the air was too swift even to allow Bill's head to be shoved forth. Von Straub clipped Bill again with the butt of the gun and had to content himself with shoving the lank body back across the bomb bay. . . .

Kip saw Greasy fall from the port and go tumbling away to vanish. In alarm she whirled to call the English lad's attention to the fact and then, turned about, she gaped in astonishment at the apparition of John Friegen who, back toward her, was trying to break loose from the grip the English lad had upon his gun hand.

The gun fired and the boy winced with shock. And then John Friegen jerked free and tried to raise the gun again. But John Friegen was trying to raise a gun which, from a normal four pounds, was suddenly jumped to thirty pounds. Kip Lee had thrown the plane into the tightest loop she could, and the centrifugal force would have rooted a fired rocket to the floor. And while they looped, the English officer twisted over on his side. Kip snapped the ship level and, in the same moment, sensing her intent, the Englishman drove his boot into John Friegen's teeth, knocking him back over the bomb compartment and making him lose his gun. It was not Marquis of Queensberry, but it worked. A second blow and the agent crumpled like an exploded paper sack.

Kip saw that the Britisher had the situation in hand and then raked the sky for a sign of the silver plane, finally finding a flash as it turned back to range alongside her.

The English lad, holding his side, and white of face, put his mouth close to her ear. "I say, that blighter announced himself as a German officer. Wouldn't attack without flying the flag, you know. Sporting, what? What shall I do with him?"

"Tie him up with something."

"What about our friend over there?" he said, pointing at the silver ship.

"We'll stick with him."

"He's waving."

Kip promptly shied out of waving distance.

Evidently unsuspecting, the silver ship banked eastward and was closely followed by Kip, who stayed a little below it.

Presently the English lad, having tied up the Nazi and then bandaged his powder burn with a section of the fellow's shirt, again leaned forward. "What now?"

"We can't load the wing guns, but there's a motor cannon."

"I should think not," he said. "But I fancy I can stuff a few into the motor cannon. You've shells?"

"Of course. This is a full military load."

"Not duds?"

"That was part of the game. No duds."

"Really, you Americans are a thorough lot!" He upended himself beside her boots and fed a belt into the 20 mm motor cannon.

"Where do you suppose he's taking us?" he queried.

"I don't know. My guess is he's trying to make Europe. Know radio?"

"Rather!"

"Then get back there and call for a position from Pan Am. That's the Atlantic down there, but what part of it we're over I don't know."

"At this rate, I think we're over considerable of it, what?" And he went to work on the radio. Presently, while his signal was going out, "Now whom do I call?"

"NC. That's our Coast Guard. I don't know what this is about, but those lads claim they're always prepared."

But for all her attempt to keep from showing concern, her hands on the stick and throttle trembled. She had begun to realize in the last few minutes that Bill Trevillian's fate, as it had always been, was a matter of terrible concern to her. And that had not been Bill who had been spilled out of the BCA's port. Ordinarily, she knew, she could cope with most anything in the air. But bullets—and Bill in that plane—!

"Righto. I've the Coast Guard. What do I say now?"

"Tell them to contact the Navy. I think I'm beginning to get the idea."

"The Navy?"

"Right."

The BCA before and above them was beginning to ease down the scale from the sixteen thousand feet which it had been holding. Kip slipped off her oxygen mask and began to watch the sea below.

"They're in a spin," said the English lad, referring to the

Coast Guard. "They want to know what's up. Shall I tell them, or is this our own show?"

"Tell them there's a Nazi ship out here waiting and to pour on the coal and get out here."

"Righto!" And the English officer returned to the radio.

And, some three minutes later, the ship came up over the horizon. It was lying to, evidently expecting them. At the most, Kip had expected a big freighter. But this vessel was long and lean and gray, and guns bristled from her decks. Kip's hand on the throttle trembled a little more. She was not quite sure even yet just what would happen, for there was no provision for landing a plane on a destroyer that she knew about.

"I say, Miss Lee! They've picked up our signals and they're telling the other chap about it!"

The English officer had hardly got the statement out before the other plane pulled up from its obvious intention of landing in the sea near the vessel and came roaring skyward, flame spouting from the guns on either side of the nose!

Kip had the advantage of altitude. All she knew of the real thing was what Terry had taught her, and while it was all right with camera guns, honest-to-Pete lead was something else.

She had an impulse to go away from there as fast as the churning prop could take her. And then she thought of Bill. What would happen to him? What *had* happened to him? And if she ran away—

A sob rose up and stuck in her throat. She looped and, upside down, dived straight at the silver plane. It dodged with a dive, and when it again pulled up, Kip was sitting on its tail. But she could not fire and risk hitting Bill. She remembered an old stunt Terry had talked about—following through above another ship in unison. That was easy with slow crates. But at five hundred and something—

And yet she forced herself to do it. She edged up and put the other plane directly under her, almost touching it. Erich von Straub sought to frighten her by pulling up. She stayed where she was, her prop within inches of sawing through the BCA 41's hood. Erich von Straub hastily dodged—and found her still with him, still almost touching him!

He looped and she looped with him. He verticaled, and she verticaled ever so slightly less. She was still with him. Stunt flying, not military flying. Stunt flying! Loop, roll—*Ach!* He dared no snap roll. She wouldn't get out of his way!

Suddenly von Straub realized that the destroyer was watching him, and from dashing all over the sky, he grew cunning. He flashed back toward the vessel and over it, suddenly diving almost into the trough of the waves. Flame and smoke chattered from the vessel's decks. Kip Lee, glancing back, saw and shied skyward. And in that moment of relief, von Straub came about and, with cut gun and opened slots, knifed in for a water landing.

It would be risky, but he had counted on that for a long time and he knew how to take chances. By keeping his wheels unlowered, he would not nosedive straight for the bottom. And there was enough air in the wings and the fuselage to float the ship, if it did not collapse—

The BCA 41 slapped a wave and rebounded. He forced it

down, and again it settled to a wave. There was a smother of foam and a wall of green, and then, hauling back the stick, von Straub sent the silver ship upward and out of the water like a flying fish. All speed was killed. Only the tip of the right wing was damaged. He bobbed to a halt about a quarter of a mile from the destroyer. Immediately it began to get out a boat and head for him.

Kip felt faint. Several dark puffs appeared far behind her and below, and she knew she was being fired upon. The flashes from the deck were white in the sunlight.

Three hundred miles at sea, and hours before rescue could come—for the fastest pursuit would still lag far behind them!

"I say," said the English lad, "I've a steamer."

"Have you got our last position?"

"Right, and it's just over the rim from us."

"Tell them to hurry!"

She stopped spiraling and straightened into a dive. The longboat was within a few hundred yards of the BCA 41 like some big shark anxious to gobble its prey. And the destroyer was creeping up. Dark blobs of smoke appeared ahead of the L97, but Kip kept going down.

She pressed the trip of the motor cannon, sighting between longboat and plane. The white line looked like a piece of thick cloth suddenly hauled, like a curtain, from the sea. The longboat sheered off.

She was gone and back, and again the water was churned and she was gone again.

The BCA 41 was beginning to settle. It would float only a

few minutes, at best. Was it better, she vainly asked herself, to let Bill be picked up by that destroyer or risk his drowning?

"I say, look there!" cried the Englishman, pointing.

She looked as she banked to go back again and found nothing. Again she sewed lead between the longboat and the plane, and the sailors in the boat showed no liking for approaching the plane. And the destroyer's machine-gun fire died.

The longboat put about and, shot along by striving backs, closed in beside the destroyer and was hastily snatched up by blocks. The vessel surged ahead and, despite the anxious waving of one Erich von Straub from the settling BCA 41, got out of there at thirty-nine knots.

Not until then did Kip see what the English officer had tried to show her. A long pale gray ship was cleaving the waves toward the spot, a great dark plume streaming out behind. And from the other direction a second ship, a freighter, was coming up with all speed. It would be some time before they converged, and the naval vessel would get there first.

Kip, hardly daring to breathe as she circled, gun cut, marking the downed plane, heard the English boy chattering madly into the radiophone. And then she experienced a wave of disappointment. The naval vessel was not going to stop! It came by the floating plane at a distance of a few yards, nearly swamping it—and all it did was throw two life jackets at it!

"You've got to keep spotting!" shouted the English officer. "They'll get her. Oh, I say, what a show when they catch her!"

And not until then did Kip understand that the naval vessel was an English cruiser.

Again she sewed lead between the longboat and the plane,
and the sailors in the boat showed no liking
for approaching the plane.

There were two puffs of white, one fore and one aft, and two seaplanes were catapulted outward from the cruiser. One leaped skyward to keep the Nazi destroyer in sight, and the other—once more Kip felt her heart begin to beat, for the other came back and made a landing beside the nearly vanished BCA 41.

She watched while they picked up two men from it and the plane again took the air. Then the English officer said, "They say he's all right, that Trevillian chap. Knocked about, but all right. They'll put him aboard and fix him up and send him back the first chance they get. Oh—oh, I *say*!"

"Can you fly?" said Kip.

"Why, yes."

"Then—then fly us home."

And she abandoned the controls to their fate and crawled over the bomb bay to sink down on the floor. She had had enough—more than enough. . . .

Six days later, having been put aboard a British freighter, Bill came home from the wars. He still wore a bandage about his brow where the gun butt had cut him, but otherwise he was all right. Long ago he had become immune to getting banged up badly.

It was all a mystery to him up to the time he had seen the Nazi destroyer going down. And to wake up and find himself in the midst of a sea battle, without any explanation whatever, had been the one thing which had preyed upon him.

He walked into the BCA office and tried to be as casual

as possible. But what he was hoping was that he could get his check and get out of there before Cannard saw him. And in that he failed. For a young English officer bounced in and greeted him as an old friend, though he couldn't recall having seen the fellow before.

"Oh, I say, that was ripping, wasn't it?"

"What?" queried Bill.

"Why, the battle, and your holding us off so well, and then von Straub and the destroyer getting caught and sunk, and Miss Lee scaring the daylights out of the boat crew and all that!"

"Miss Lee? Kip?"

"Certainly! Why, she hung on like a terrier to a rat until she was sure you were out of it!"

"Now look!" said Bill. "It's no fair to jump into the middle of a story this way. We were camera-scrapping, and then—?"

"Oh, so you were out of it, eh? Well now—" And with keen relish, the officer reeled it off—with many gestures. A whole hour of it. Bill sat dumbfounded.

"So that," said Bill, when the lad had finished, "is what it was all about! And Kip stuck by and kept away the longboat and— *Gosh!*"

"Oh, quite a stunt, I assure you!"

"No. You don't get it—you don't get it at all! She loves me!"

"Obviously," said the English boy.

"Say, have you got a car? Would you drive me someplace?"

"Glad to."

The cashier had come in and had thrust something into Bill's hand, but he didn't look at it. He clutched it, unfelt, all the way to Calver and even failed to notice it when Terry Lee gladly gripped his hand.

"Where's Kip?" demanded Bill.

"Oh, I guess she's around. We didn't know when you'd be here or we'd have had a celebration. A quiet one, you know. The thing hasn't leaked out. A black eye to the FBI, and a lot of panic about sabotage and so forth, you know. And no harm done. Greasy, have you seen Kip?"

Greasy got up off the steps and grinned at Bill.

"*Greasy!* What are *you* doing here?" said Bill.

"I work here. Since Terry got the contract, he needed some help."

"Oh, so you got the contract!" said Bill, but one could see his heart wasn't in it. He was fidgeting to get away from them—and very soon did.

Down in the storage hangar he found a pair of overalled legs sticking out from under a wing. "Hey, down there! Have you seen Kip?"

She wriggled out, wrench in hand, wiping the smudge of grease from her nose with the back of her left—only making it worse.

"*Bill!*"

He just stood looking at her in adoration.

She wiped off her hands on her overalls. "I don't trust a mech anymore. Besides, about forty-leven years ago you taught me how. I guess I'm a sight."

"You're the only sight I've wanted to see for an age."

She looked wonderingly at him. "Gee, Bill! Do you really mean that?"

"You bet I do!" He reached for her. But she backed up.

"You still think, after that show I put on for you, that dames can't fly?"

Guiltily he lied. "That was the swellest show any pilot ever put over. I remember every twist of it. Look, do you still think I'm a saboteur?"

"I never thought you were. I just said that. Bill, I tried for six years to get as good as you were and then you said I couldn't fly worth beans, and gee—I had an awful time proving it!"

"Then," and he felt suddenly sad, "you were just proving a point?"

"You bet I was. Because the only girl you'd ever look at twice would be one that could fly as good as you could. Do I win?"

"You win," said Bill.

And when he put his arms about her he suddenly found himself staring at a check for thirteen thousand dollars. Three thousand pay. Ten thousand bonus for landing the contract.

"Look!" he cried. "They must have split it!"

"They did. Five hundred planes of each type."

"And then—hell's skyways! Thirteen thousand dollars! All in one chunk and nothing to do? I tell you. We'll buy a plane. We'll buy a cabin plane and we'll get married and fly someplace."

"You mean it, Bill?"

"Well, don't *bawl* about it!"

"I . . . I gotta bawl! When you've worked for something for years and years and it all comes true . . . I just gotta bawl, Bill!"

Story Preview

NOW that you've just ventured through one of the captivating tales in the Stories from the Golden Age collection by L. Ron Hubbard, turn the page and enjoy a preview of *The Sky-Crasher*. Join Caution Jones, a man who, despite his nickname, risks the hazards of a breathtaking, around-the-world flight while a rival airline desperately tries to sabotage his every move.

The Sky-Crasher

CRAIG, hair bushy and stiff as steel wool, his face the color of raw beef, entered with a militant stride and thumped himself onto the edge of the desk.

"What's this note you sent me?" demanded Craig. "You don't like this world flight?"

"No," said Caution. "That's what I'm paid to do."

"What?"

"See that TCA keeps going."

"But look at that potential earning!"

"United States Airlines," said Caution, with a shake of his head, "is going in for this thing. And they're after our scalps. They're buying up our stocks, cutting our rates and shortening our schedules. Mercer is going to hammer us into the middle of next week. And if Mercer and United States Airlines don't want us in that race, they'll see that we stay out, or kill our pilot."

"Nuts!" said Craig.

"And," said Caution, "we're almost on the rocks. We can barely keep running."

Craig sat up, astonished, blowing hard. "Why didn't you tell me?"

"My job is to keep you from working hard, isn't it? You have enough to worry you. But you can look at our ledgers. We're running in the red, and if things don't pick up, TCA will disappear from the skyways. All the work you and I have done will be gone. Wrecked. We're lucky to be going at all. We need every pilot to keep us in the air. We need every penny to keep the planes in the air. We *can't* afford to make that flight."

"Who said so?"

Caution looked very official, very earnest. "United States Airlines is trying to push us out. If we enter this race—call it yellow if you want—we'll lose out. We don't play the game crooked, and they do."

Craig took the wrapper off a cigar and then began to gnaw upon it as a dog gnaws a bone. He considered Caution for several seconds, speculation in his eye.

"Caution," said Craig, "if I didn't know you better, I'd say you *were* yellow."

Caution took it without a blink. "You pay me to say these things and do these things, not to stunt and romp around like a colt."

"Sure, sure, I know. But listen here, Caution, I've always wondered just what the hell was wrong with you. Now don't get me wrong. You're a crack pilot and you've got a fine business head. But what's under all this?"

Caution's lean face changed. His mouth drew down on one side, his left eye closed ever so little. The expression completely transformed him. It was bitter, reckless. Craig was startled. He had never seen Caution look that way before.

"You want to know the truth?" said Caution. "My dad was Batty Jones. Did you know that?"

"Why—why, yes, I'd heard of it. He was a famous circus pilot, wasn't he?" the TCA man asked.

"Yes," said Caution, biting off the word. "A famous circus pilot, nothing more. They called him Batty. He *was* batty. He grew up out of the war. He didn't give a damn for anything, not even my mother's feelings or my future. He was a *stunt* pilot.

"He starred with the old Bates Flying Circus, the craziest fools aviation ever bred. He came out of the JN-9 era and flew himself up into the money and fame. He was the idol of all kids. He didn't have a nerve in his body. He looked like me, but that's where the resemblance ended.

"One time, off Florida, he flew down a twenty-foot alley with a plane which spread its wings forty feet. One time he wrecked ships, diving them straight in from thousands of feet, just to give the crowd a thrill. One time he arranged with a pilot so that they'd smash their ships together in midair just to amuse the mob. They did it, and the other pilot died. Batty Jones got out with a busted arm and a scratched ear.

"His stunts were famous. Anything for a stunt. Anything for a thrill. He lived hard and high and fast. He was the best pilot in the world, and he turned that talent into money by amusing people, by giving them chills. He was a *stunt* pilot, get me?"

Craig sat very still, amazed at Caution's wild tone. Caution got up and paced down the room, scowling, eye squinted, mouth drawn bitterly down.

"He wouldn't fly sanely. He wouldn't give aviation a break. No, he dangled off wings, looped ships ready to fall apart, parachuted, cracked up, burned in the air and came out of it every time, grinning.

"A circus pilot. They didn't last long. In 1928 my dad burned the ship in the air, figuring that he could bail out in his chute. A wing hit him when it folded. I watched him burn a thousand feet above the earth. I thought it was just another stunt until I . . . until they . . .

"My mother was worn out with it. The final shock killed her. I greased ships, stole rides, stole time, licked boots, begged an education in the air. And I ordered myself to keep sane and steady. I had to do it, and I've done it. I'm 'Caution' Jones, the levelest head in the business."

As though suddenly tired, he sat down. When he lit a cigarette, Craig saw that his hand was shaking. He'd never seen Caution like that before.

"Then," said Craig, after a long pause, "I guess we don't want to try that round-the-world flight. You're right, Caution, it's a stunt. No reason to do it. But still—we've got to get out of this hole somehow. I've put my life into TCA, you've given it years yourself. It's all we've got. And we don't want to take a beating lying down just because a gang of crooks like United States Airlines tries to muscle in on it.

"However, we'll find something else, something less spectacular. The round-the-world flight is out."

Unseen by both, the silver ship which had lately been stunting over the field had landed. A slim, booted figure had stepped out, and now that person was standing in the doorway, looking at them.

To find out more about *The Sky-Crasher* and how you can obtain your copy, go to www.goldenagestories.com.

Glossary

STORIES FROM THE GOLDEN AGE *reflect the words and expressions used in the 1930s and 1940s, adding unique flavor and authenticity to the tales. While a character's speech may often reflect regional origins, it also can convey attitudes common in the day. So that readers can better grasp such cultural and historical terms, uncommon words or expressions of the era, the following glossary has been provided.*

---

aileron: a hinged flap on the trailing edge of an aircraft wing, used to control banking movements.

altimeter: a gauge that measures altitude.

altocirrus: wispy white clouds, usually of fine ice crystals, at an altitude of 7,000 to 25,000 feet (2,100 to 7,600 meters). Also used figuratively.

altocumulus: medium-sized puffy, patchy, scattered clouds, often in linear bands.

ammeters: instruments for measuring electric current.

ASI: airspeed indicator.

banshee: (Irish legend) a female spirit whose wailing warns of a death in a house.

barograph: an instrument that continuously records changes in atmospheric pressure on a piece of paper mounted on a rotating cylinder.

blighter: a person regarded with contempt.

Bowden: Bowden wire; a type of flexible wire used to transmit a pulling force over a short distance (such as the remote shutter release cables on a film camera).

Bowie: horse racetrack built in Bowie, Maryland in 1914 (no longer active).

camera guns: aircraft-mounted motion picture cameras that record the firing of the guns and their target line as aimed by the pilot.

Chinese rat torture: torture whereby a rat was placed on the victim's stomach with a small metallic container placed over it. The torturer would heat the container, making the rat dig its way out.

cowl: a removable metal covering for an engine, especially an aircraft engine.

crate: an airplane.

Dornier: Dornier DO 17, sometimes referred to as "the Pencil" due to its fundamental shape, was a twin-engine medium-size bomber utilized by the Germans during World War II.

drink of water: a very tall, thin person.

forty-leven: an expression used to describe a huge number.

Gates: Gates Flying Circus, founded by Major Ivan Gates in 1922, was one of the most famous barnstorming shows of the time. Some of the greatest stunt fliers worked for

Gates, including Clyde "Upside-Down" Pangborn, who specialized in flying upside down and changing planes in midair.

G-men: government men; agents of the Federal Bureau of Investigation.

greaseball: a worker who lubricates the working parts of a machine or vehicle.

ground loop: to cause an aircraft to ground loop, or make a sharp horizontal turn when taxiing, landing or taking off.

het up: upset.

"hot papas": personnel whose duty it is to rescue people from burning aircraft. They wear protective suits, formerly made of asbestos, to safeguard them so they can work close to burning planes.

JN-9: Curtiss N-9; a seaplane used to train US Navy pilots during World War I. The N-9 was used in 1916 and 1917 for the development of ship-mounted launch catapults and flight testing the new autopilot components intended to be used in pilotless "aerial torpedoes." They were retired by the Navy in 1927.

Lewis: a double-barreled Lewis antiaircraft machine gun based on the gas-operated machine gun designed by US Army Colonel Isaac Newton Lewis. In 1911, Lewis designed a machine gun that weighed about half as much as a typical machine gun. The lightness of the gun made it popular in the field and as an aircraft-mounted weapon, especially since the cooling effect of the high-speed air over the gun meant that the gun's cooling mechanisms could be removed, making the weapon even lighter.

longboat: the longest boat carried by a sailing ship.

lying to: stopping with the vessel heading into the wind.

Marquis of Queensberry: referring to the official rules for the sport of boxing; originated by John Sholto Douglas (1844–1900), a British nobleman and eighth Marquis of Queensberry (a hill in lower Scotland).

Messerschmitt: a famous German aircraft manufacturer known primarily for its World War II fighter aircraft. In 1927, Willy Messerschmitt joined the company, then known as Bavarian Aircraft Works, as chief designer. He promoted a new lightweight design in which many separate parts were merged into a single reinforced firewall, thereby saving weight and improving performance. The Messerschmitt became a favorite of the German government and in 1938 the company was renamed with Willy Messerschmitt as chairman.

Messerschmitt 109F: German World War II fighter aircraft designed by Willy Messerschmitt in the early 1930s. It was one of the first true modern fighters of the era with all-metal construction, a closed canopy and retractable landing gear. With its new lightweight construction and improved performance, the aircraft won the German air force fighter contest in 1935 and soon thereafter became a favorite of the German government.

monoplane: an airplane with one sustaining surface or one set of wings.

motor cannon: a type of gun that shoots through the propeller hub of a fighter plane.

NC: North Carolina; US Coast Guard Air Station located in

Elizabeth City, North Carolina, on the Pasquotank River near the Atlantic coast. The air station was commissioned in August 1940 and was initially equipped with three seaplanes, three amphibians and four landplanes. It was established for its potential strategic value as a seaplane base and was utilized during World War II under US Navy control for Search and Rescue (SAR), anti-submarine and training missions.

Pan Am: Pan American World Airways, the principal international airline of the United States from the 1930s until it closed its operations in 1991. Originally founded as a seaplane service out of Florida, the airline became a major company credited with many innovations that shaped the international airline industry.

plaster of Paris: a white powder that when mixed with water forms a quick-hardening paste. It is used in the arts for sculpting and making casts, and in medicine for molding casts around broken limbs.

Prussian: in the manner of a military officer from Prussia. Prussia, a former northern European nation, based much of its rule on armed might, stressing rigid military discipline and maintaining one of the most strictly drilled armies in the world.

ring mount: a rotating mount on an aircraft that allowed the gun to be turned to any direction with the gunner remaining directly behind it.

ripping: (British informal) excellent.

roadster: an open-top automobile with a single seat in front for two or three persons, a fabric top and either a luggage compartment or a rumble seat in back. A rumble seat is an upholstered exterior seat with a hinged lid that opens to form the back of the seat when in use.

rudder: a device used to steer ships or aircraft. A rudder is a flat plane or sheet of material attached with hinges to the craft's stern or tail. In typical aircraft, pedals operate rudders via mechanical linkages.

Scheherazade: the female narrator of *The Arabian Nights,* who during one thousand and one adventurous nights saved her life by entertaining her husband, the king, with stories.

seat-stick: a walking stick with handles at one end that fold out to form a small seat.

slipped: sideslip; (of an aircraft when excessively banked) to slide sideways, toward the center of the curve described in turning.

slipstream: the airstream pushed back by a revolving aircraft propeller.

snap roll: a maneuver in which an aircraft makes a single quick revolution about its longitudinal axis while flying horizontally.

stall: a situation in which an aircraft suddenly dives because the airflow is obstructed and lift is lost. The loss of airflow can be caused by insufficient airspeed or by an excessive angle of an airfoil (part of an aircraft's surface that provides lift or control) when the aircraft is climbing.

tab: a small, adjustable hinged surface, located on the trailing edge of the aileron, rudder or elevator control surface; also called *trim tab*. It is adjusted by the pilot to maintain balance and to help stabilize the aircraft in flight.

tach: tachometer; a device used to determine speed of rotation, typically of an engine's crankshaft, usually measured in revolutions per minute.

tarmac: airport runway.

terminal velocity: the constant speed that a falling object reaches when the downward gravitational force equals the frictional resistance of the medium through which it is falling, usually air.

Teuton: a native of Germany or a person of German origin.

three points: three-point landing; an airplane landing in which the two main wheels and the nose wheel all touch the ground simultaneously.

turtleback: the part of the airplane behind the cockpit that is shaped like the back of a turtle.

Udet: Ernst Udet (1896–1941), the second-highest-scoring German flying ace of World War I, with sixty-two victories.

whipstall: a maneuver in a small aircraft in which it goes into a vertical climb, pauses briefly, and then drops toward the earth, nose first.

Winchell, Walter: American journalist whose newspaper column "On Broadway" (1924–1963) and radio newscasts (1932–1953) reported on entertainment and politics.

wind tee: a large weathervane shaped like an airplane, or a horizontal letter T, located on or near a landing field, to indicate wind direction to airplane pilots.

windward: facing the wind or on the side facing the wind.

wing walking: the act of moving on the wings of an airplane during flight. Wing walkers were barnstormers who were the ultimate risk takers of their day. Performing stunts on the wings of a plane during flight started in 1917 when a US Army pilot climbed out on the wing of his plane while in mid-air to resolve certain problems. This act boosted morale and confidence in his fellow pilots, and as a result, the art of wing walking took off.

wooden nickels, don't take any: take care of yourself; goodbye and watch yourself. Used as an amiable parting salutation.

L. Ron Hubbard
in the Golden Age
of Pulp Fiction

*In writing an adventure story
a writer has to know that he is adventuring
for a lot of people who cannot.
The writer has to take them here and there
about the globe and show them
excitement and love and realism.
As long as that writer is living the part of an
adventurer when he is hammering
the keys, he is succeeding with his story.*

*Adventuring is a state of mind.
If you adventure through life, you have a
good chance to be a success on paper.*

*Adventure doesn't mean globe-trotting,
exactly, and it doesn't mean great deeds.
Adventuring is like art.
You have to live it to make it real.*

— *L. RON HUBBARD*

L. Ron Hubbard
and American
Pulp Fiction

B ORN March 13, 1911, L. Ron Hubbard lived a life at least as expansive as the stories with which he enthralled a hundred million readers through a fifty-year career.

Originally hailing from Tilden, Nebraska, he spent his formative years in a classically rugged Montana, replete with the cowpunchers, lawmen and desperadoes who would later people his Wild West adventures. And lest anyone imagine those adventures were drawn from vicarious experience, he was not only breaking broncs at a tender age, he was also among the few whites ever admitted into Blackfoot society as a bona fide blood brother. While if only to round out an otherwise rough and tumble youth, his mother was that rarity of her time—a thoroughly educated woman—who introduced her son to the classics of Occidental literature even before his seventh birthday.

But as any dedicated L. Ron Hubbard reader will attest, his world extended far beyond Montana. In point of fact, and as the son of a United States naval officer, by the age of eighteen he had traveled over a quarter of a million miles. Included therein were three Pacific crossings to a then still mysterious Asia, where he ran with the likes of Her British Majesty's agent-in-place

L. Ron Hubbard, left, at Congressional Airport, Washington, DC, 1931, with members of George Washington University flying club.

for North China, and the last in the line of Royal Magicians from the court of Kublai Khan. For the record, L. Ron Hubbard was also among the first Westerners to gain admittance to forbidden Tibetan monasteries below Manchuria, and his photographs of China's Great Wall long graced American geography texts.

Upon his return to the United States and a hasty completion of his interrupted high school education, the young Ron Hubbard entered George Washington University. There, as fans of his aerial adventures may have heard, he earned his wings as a pioneering barnstormer at the dawn of American aviation. He also earned a place in free-flight record books for the longest sustained flight above Chicago. Moreover, as a roving reporter for *Sportsman Pilot* (featuring his first professionally penned articles), he further helped inspire a generation of pilots who would take America to world airpower.

Immediately beyond his sophomore year, Ron embarked on the first of his famed ethnological expeditions, initially to then untrammeled Caribbean shores (descriptions of which would later fill a whole series of West Indies mystery-thrillers). That the Puerto Rican interior would also figure into the future of Ron Hubbard stories was likewise no accident. For in addition to cultural studies of the island, a 1932–33

LRH expedition is rightly remembered as conducting the first complete mineralogical survey of a Puerto Rico under United States jurisdiction.

There was many another adventure along this vein: As a lifetime member of the famed Explorers Club, L. Ron Hubbard charted North Pacific waters with the first shipboard radio direction finder, and so pioneered a long-range navigation system universally employed until the late twentieth century. While not to put too fine an edge on it, he also held a rare Master Mariner's license to pilot any vessel, of any tonnage in any ocean.

Yet lest we stray too far afield, there is an LRH note at this juncture in his saga, and it reads in part:

"I started out writing for the pulps, writing the best I knew, writing for every mag on the stands, slanting as well as I could."

To which one might add: His earliest submissions date from the summer of 1934, and included tales drawn from true-to-life Asian adventures, with characters roughly modeled on British/American intelligence operatives he had known in Shanghai. His early Westerns were similarly peppered with details drawn from personal experience. Although therein lay a first hard lesson from the often cruel world of the pulps. His first Westerns were soundly rejected as lacking the authenticity of a Max Brand yarn

Capt. L. Ron Hubbard in Ketchikan, Alaska, 1940, on his Alaskan Radio Experimental Expedition, the first of three voyages conducted under the Explorers Club flag.

(a particularly frustrating comment given L. Ron Hubbard's Westerns came straight from his Montana homeland, while Max Brand was a mediocre New York poet named Frederick Schiller Faust, who turned out implausible six-shooter tales from the terrace of an Italian villa).

Nevertheless, and needless to say, L. Ron Hubbard persevered and soon earned a reputation as among the most publishable names in pulp fiction, with a ninety percent placement rate of first-draft manuscripts. He was also among the most prolific, averaging between seventy and a hundred thousand words a month. Hence the rumors that L. Ron Hubbard had redesigned a typewriter for faster keyboard action and pounded out manuscripts on a continuous roll of butcher paper to save the precious seconds it took to insert a single sheet of paper into manual typewriters of the day.

That all L. Ron Hubbard stories did not run beneath said byline is yet another aspect of pulp fiction lore. That is, as publishers periodically rejected manuscripts from top-drawer authors if only to avoid paying top dollar, L. Ron Hubbard and company just as frequently replied with submissions under various pseudonyms. In Ron's case, the

A MAN OF MANY NAMES

Between 1934 and 1950, L. Ron Hubbard authored more than fifteen million words of fiction in more than two hundred classic publications. To supply his fans and editors with stories across an array of genres and pulp titles, he adopted fifteen pseudonyms in addition to his already renowned L. Ron Hubbard byline.

Winchester Remington Colt
Lt. Jonathan Daly
Capt. Charles Gordon
Capt. L. Ron Hubbard
Bernard Hubbel
Michael Keith
Rene Lafayette
Legionnaire 148
Legionnaire 14830
Ken Martin
Scott Morgan
Lt. Scott Morgan
Kurt von Rachen
Barry Randolph
Capt. Humbert Reynolds

list included: Rene Lafayette, Captain Charles Gordon, Lt. Scott Morgan and the notorious Kurt von Rachen—supposedly on the lam for a murder rap, while hammering out two-fisted prose in Argentina. The point: While L. Ron Hubbard as Ken Martin spun stories of Southeast Asian intrigue, LRH as Barry Randolph authored tales of

L. Ron Hubbard, circa 1930, at the outset of a literary career that would finally span half a century.

romance on the Western range—which, stretching between a dozen genres is how he came to stand among the two hundred elite authors providing close to a million tales through the glory days of American Pulp Fiction.

In evidence of exactly that, by 1936 L. Ron Hubbard was literally leading pulp fiction's elite as president of New York's American Fiction Guild. Members included a veritable pulp hall of fame: Lester "Doc Savage" Dent, Walter "The Shadow" Gibson, and the legendary Dashiell Hammett—to cite but a few.

Also in evidence of just where L. Ron Hubbard stood within his first two years on the American pulp circuit: By the spring of 1937, he was ensconced in Hollywood, adopting a Caribbean thriller for Columbia Pictures, remembered today as *The Secret of Treasure Island*. Comprising fifteen thirty-minute episodes, the L. Ron Hubbard screenplay led to the most profitable matinée serial in Hollywood history. In accord with Hollywood culture, he was thereafter continually called upon

The 1937 Secret of Treasure Island, *a fifteen-episode serial adapted for the screen by L. Ron Hubbard from his novel,* Murder at Pirate Castle.

to rewrite/doctor scripts—most famously for long-time friend and fellow adventurer Clark Gable.

In the interim—and herein lies another distinctive chapter of the L. Ron Hubbard story—he continually worked to open Pulp Kingdom gates to up-and-coming authors. Or, for that matter, anyone who wished to write. It was a fairly unconventional stance, as markets were already thin and competition razor sharp. But the fact remains, it was an L. Ron Hubbard hallmark that he vehemently lobbied on behalf of young authors—regularly supplying instructional articles to trade journals, guest-lecturing to short story classes at George Washington University and Harvard, and even founding his own creative writing competition. It was established in 1940, dubbed the Golden Pen, and guaranteed winners both New York representation and publication in *Argosy*.

But it was John W. Campbell Jr.'s *Astounding Science Fiction* that finally proved the most memorable LRH vehicle. While every fan of L. Ron Hubbard's galactic epics undoubtedly knows the story, it nonetheless bears repeating: By late 1938, the pulp publishing magnate of Street & Smith was determined to revamp *Astounding Science Fiction* for broader readership. In particular, senior editorial director F. Orlin Tremaine called for stories with a stronger *human element*. When acting editor John W. Campbell balked, preferring his spaceship-driven tales, Tremaine enlisted Hubbard. Hubbard, in turn, replied with the genre's first truly *character-driven* works, wherein heroes are pitted not against bug-eyed monsters but the mystery and majesty of deep space itself—and thus was launched the Golden Age of Science Fiction.

The names alone are enough to quicken the pulse of any science fiction aficionado, including LRH friend and protégé, Robert Heinlein, Isaac Asimov, A. E. van Vogt and Ray Bradbury. Moreover, when coupled with LRH stories of fantasy, we further come to what's rightly been described as the foundation of every modern tale of horror: L. Ron Hubbard's immortal *Fear*. It was rightly proclaimed by Stephen King as one of the very few works to genuinely warrant that overworked term "classic"—as in: *"This is a classic tale of creeping, surreal menace and horror. . . . This is one of the really, really good ones."*

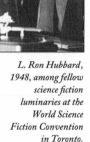

L. Ron Hubbard, 1948, among fellow science fiction luminaries at the World Science Fiction Convention in Toronto.

To accommodate the greater body of L. Ron Hubbard fantasies, Street & Smith inaugurated *Unknown*—a classic pulp if there ever was one, and wherein readers were soon thrilling to the likes of *Typewriter in the Sky* and *Slaves of Sleep* of which Frederik Pohl would declare: *"There are bits and pieces from Ron's work that became part of the language in ways that very few other writers managed."*

And, indeed, at J. W. Campbell Jr.'s insistence, Ron was regularly drawing on themes from the Arabian Nights and so introducing readers to a world of genies, jinn, Aladdin and Sinbad—all of which, of course, continue to float through cultural mythology to this day.

At least as influential in terms of post-apocalypse stories was L. Ron Hubbard's 1940 *Final Blackout*. Generally acclaimed as the finest anti-war novel of the decade and among the ten best works of the genre ever authored—here, too, was a tale that would live on in ways few other writers imagined.

Hence, the later Robert Heinlein verdict: "Final Blackout *is as perfect a piece of science fiction as has ever been written.*"

Like many another who both lived and wrote American pulp adventure, the war proved a tragic end to Ron's sojourn in the pulps. He served with distinction in four theaters and was highly decorated for commanding corvettes in the North Pacific. He was also grievously wounded in combat, lost many a close friend and colleague and thus resolved to say farewell to pulp fiction and devote himself to what it had supported these many years—namely, his serious research.

Portland, Oregon, 1943; L. Ron Hubbard, captain of the US Navy subchaser PC 815.

But in no way was the LRH literary saga at an end, for as he wrote some thirty years later, in 1980:

"Recently there came a period when I had little to do. This was novel in a life so crammed with busy years, and I decided to amuse myself by writing a novel that was pure *science fiction."*

That work was *Battlefield Earth: A Saga of the Year 3000*. It was an immediate *New York Times* bestseller and, in fact, the first international science fiction blockbuster in decades. It was not, however, L. Ron Hubbard's magnum opus, as that distinction is generally reserved for his next and final work: The 1.2 million word *Mission Earth*.

> **Final Blackout**
> *is as perfect*
> *a piece of*
> *science fiction*
> *as has ever*
> *been written.*
>
> —Robert Heinlein

How he managed those 1.2 million words in just over twelve months is yet another piece of the L. Ron Hubbard legend. But the fact remains, he did indeed author a ten-volume *dekalogy* that lives in publishing history for the fact that each and every volume of the series was also a *New York Times* bestseller.

Moreover, as subsequent generations discovered L. Ron Hubbard through republished works and novelizations of his screenplays, the mere fact of his name on a cover signaled an international bestseller. . . . Until, to date, sales of his works exceed hundreds of millions, and he otherwise remains among the most enduring and widely read authors in literary history. Although as a final word on the tales of L. Ron Hubbard, perhaps it's enough to simply reiterate what editors told readers in the glory days of American Pulp Fiction:

He writes the way he does, brothers, because he's been there, seen it and done it!

THE STORIES FROM THE GOLDEN AGE

Your ticket to adventure starts here with the Stories from
the Golden Age collection by master storyteller L. Ron Hubbard.
These gripping tales are set in a kaleidoscope of exotic locales and brim
with fascinating characters, including some of the
most vile villains, dangerous dames and brazen heroes
you'll ever get to meet.

The entire collection of over one hundred and fifty stories is being
released in a series of eighty books and audiobooks.
For an up-to-date listing of available titles,
go to www.goldenagestories.com.

AIR ADVENTURE

Arctic Wings	*Man-Killers of the Air*
The Battling Pilot	*On Blazing Wings*
Boomerang Bomber	*Red Death Over China*
The Crate Killer	*Sabotage in the Sky*
The Dive Bomber	*Sky Birds Dare!*
Forbidden Gold	*The Sky-Crasher*
Hurtling Wings	*Trouble on His Wings*
The Lieutenant Takes the Sky	*Wings Over Ethiopia*

FAR-FLUNG ADVENTURE

SEA ADVENTURE

TALES FROM THE ORIENT

MYSTERY

FANTASY

SCIENCE FICTION

WESTERN

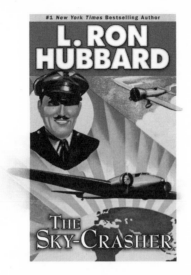